ON CALL

DEDICATED TO MY SON,
WILLIAM HUNT

Shelby Fire Chief William Hunt has been named North Carolina 2021 Career Fire Chief of the Year. Hunt has served in the role for 14 years. A native of Lexington, he has spent more than three decades in fire service.

ON CALL

ROTHA J. DAWKINS

ReadersMagnet, LLC

CHAPTER ONE

The Chief stopped into the firehouse. A-Company was sitting at a long table beginning their Sunday evening meal. Family and friends joined them with bringing food and conversation.

"Did you hear the weather report" Chief Jerry Thomas inquired.

A seven-year-old son of one fireman cut in, "We've got to eat! My tum to pray."

All eyes were on him as he bowed his head smiling. He continued, "Good food, good meat; good God let's eat!"

The women gasp and stared at the child. Grinning, he reached for a tray of fried Chicken. Somehow he slipped by a scolding while everyone filled their plates. The Chief joined in. At the firehouse formal invitations weren't needed, it was always open house. Today's chicken, potato salad, hot rolls, with different jellies warm the heart and soul.

The tall truck bay doors began to rattle from the hard blowing whistling wind. Captain Williams shuddered, "It's getting real cold. We need to get a move on and put the chains on the truck tires."

"Maybe not," injected the crew commander. He burped repulsively. "That's a lot of trouble you know."

Chief Jerry Thomas mashed a big square button on a weather box in front of him. Everybody listened.

The box immediately began a continual report. It was saying, "There are 40 to 50 m.p.h. winds expected through the night and early morning with possible gusts of more than 60 m.p.h. Temperature will drop just below zero. Light rain will freeze making all driving very hazardous. Guard yourself cautiously if you are to be out doors. Take care of animals to not let them get exposed. Tomorrow, winds will shift from the North."

"That's it! We must be ready. With all this freeze, somebody will have an attic fire or something," Captain Williams cautioned.

Once the meal was finished, the visitors departed quickly to beat the storm. Williams and his partner rushed to their monster ladder truck and began to set the tire chains into place.

"What are you fellows doing that for?" groaned their immediate supervisor, Commander Bailey, "We don't need chains. That's just useless, we ain't used them in years. Look at that rust there on them."

"I'd rather need and have them than to not have them and need them." Rendered the young Captain. "Pull it Todd, now lock it in place."

"Whatever you think," Bailey shook his head and moaned.

Once the boss disappeared Todd whispered, "One of these days that jerk is going to let something major happen. I just stepped outside and nearly slid down the block."

"He's too careless with my life. Want to chain all eight trucks?" Williams asked.

"Sure! Somebody needs to."

The two had been fire partners since joining the force eight years prior. Both kept up with all seminars and studies. They read everything regarding their serious profession. Each phase of their practice was updated; from jumping from buildings, practice fires, to new equipment. They lived to look after each other and go that extra mile for life.

"It's really cold. I'll get our heavy coats and gloves." Said Todd as he reached into their truck. "Here Will, take yours."

As they added the warmth and continued the chains, the commander returned. He snapped, "You boys don't let up! I told you we do not need all these trucks chained! Finish that one and forget the rest." He went outside again to his car.

Williams and Todd watched him through the glass of the bay doors. He placed a square dark bottle to his mouth and turned it up. They could see his throat move with a chugging motion. The two shook their heads and returned to their task.

Once the kitchen was back in order, the firefighters returned to the long table for coffee. This firehouse was also housing a full crew from East Side.

Their building was undergoing renovations. While they assembled, the box-radio continued warnings of the oncoming storm. The assignments for the house chores and work details were given by Captain Williams.

Commander Bailey waltzed in whistling; then he belched loudly. "I remember the days when this town had one truck and ten volunteers. Everybody knew what to do. It was all instinct. The city ought to cut the crew sizes. There's a lot of sitting around and you boys just go over the same old stuff."

"Hey Bailey," Capt. Hall from East Side scored, "This city has changed needs. You'll retire soon, things will go on."

"Yeah, I'll retire. They're counting the days." The nearly sixty-year old man answered bitterly. The department had become his target for all his mounting problems.

As one man had complained to the Fire Chief, 'He's becoming dangerous; It's as if he thrills at sending us inside a mess. He'll put us inside after it's too late to enter. I'm afraid of what can happen!'

The phone rang. "Commander Bailey, it's for you."

"Bailey, here." He listened then exploded, "What else do you want? Blood? You'll get your damn money!"

Slamming the phone against the block wall, he staggered down the hall toward his bedroom muttering, "Ex wives! That's another pile. After ten years she has two more payments, she won't ever let up!"

The door slammed shaking the walls.

The two crews began to put away their laptops and card games. The nights' movie had ended. With everything in order, each firefighter was seeking the comfort of his bed. They could hear the distant radio repeat the weather report but the temperature had changed to ten below zero.

"Night!" yelled Williams.

"Good night, John Boy!" teased Todd.

From the last room down the hall the voice of the newest recruit screamed, "Son of a gun! What's this? You idiot, you've short- sheeted my bed! Dang it! Who did this? I'll have to make it up again!"

In the semi-darkness, snickering began. Joe Todd whispered, "Wait for his light to turn on!"

Immediately, the hallway lit up. The young firefighter laughed, "Well ain't y'all sweet! Pink sheets! Well look at this ... that's the prettiest lace on them. You know how to hurt a fellow!"

Todd came to his aid and slapped him on the shoulder "Yeah, brother, you have to be initiated. Look, just grab the pink sheet out."

As they laughed together, someone yelled, "Shut up! Quiet!"

"Yes, Mommy!" squeaked Todd in a joking high-pitched voice.

Small noises interrupted what should have been solitude. Soon came the snoring with the trickling rain and pecking ice against the windows. The gusts of wind were worse than it's howling. At exactly 11:05 the big horn blast its beaconing call. The call was master.

Without hesitation, each firefighter rolled from his bed and struggled into his waiting turnout gear. Each raced to his position at his truck. Orders were announced through the overhead speakers along with continual signaling blasts. The huge bay doors raised automatically while each truck was started and made ready to depart with the waiting word from Dispatcher.

The instant the command was received; the fire trucks began the tremendous scream for their place on the slick street. Destination was the White Lumber Company about a mile from the Station. Color was already visible in the sky from the fast growing flames. The building was full of hazardous materials, aged wood, sawdust and debris from over fifty years of business. To add more fuel to the flames, the business was strolled in a hap-hazard manner over more than a city block. Full bays of lumber, plywood, roofing, plastics and all the varied hardware and lumber devices were now at total risk.

Capt. Williams arrived at the scene first with his truck and crew. As he jumped from his machine, he had to determine where to start the fire lines. He was the on-scene commander until another official might relieve him.

As the other trucks arrived, the firefighters expertly rigged their gear as he ordered. There seemed to be a sea of red flashing light intermittently with blue as the full infantry assembled to THE CALL.

A young firefighter started running toward Capt. Williams waving his arms. "Get down!" ordered Williams.

The fellow ducked just in time for a heavy water line to pass over him. "Captain! Two of the main trucks wrecked after they left the station house on the way here!"

"I wondered what happened… We need them! We have to have them if they have to tow them here," Williams flipped. " Hold on a minute."

The Captain placed the next arriving men and equipment in order for them to begin their task to tackle the roaring fire. The heat was almost overwhelming; he had to force the lines to move backward. He spoke to the young man again, " Those trucks …. two?'"

"Yes, they couldn't stop on the ice, no chains! They ran into each other." Get back to the station and help there. Check out those wrecked rigs. Tell them our radios aren't clear. Communications are all but down!" He winched. "Find the Chief!"

"Go? How?" The guy asked.

"Dang it! Take a cab or a cop! Yeah … him!" Captain pointed to a police car and motioned. "Please take this man to the station house. No, wait a second! You go for me; we need him here. Find the Chief or commander; tell them our communications are fouled up. It's probably the freezing cold. They can get a backup unit. Hurry! Go!"

The sleek Dalmatian sprang into his place to guard the trucks, He always rode #27. Mac loved all calls.

Lines were at full force with every firefighter heeding his call of direction. The weather was getting worse. Even with all the engines and available firefighters there was still very little happening that seemed to subdue any flames. Fire spread inside and materials began blasting off and spraying its residue. It only brought about more risk and trouble.

Williams called out to Todd, "We've got to get on top of this thing. It's the only way. Here comes the Chief now!"

Chief Thomas agreed getting above the inferno was the only way to really start knocking down the flames and stop the fire from jumping around.

Chief wiped his wet face and held his hand out, "Area fire departments are on alert and coming. Two of our units wrecked coming here. Men had to go to the hospital too. Commander Bailey was driving one. Sure glad you jumped in to replace his post. He's something!"

"Chief; get someone else here with you. Todd and I need to get up there. Nobody can get inside. It's totally engulfed on the ground. We can get up there."

"Go! You know what to do. Take this walkie-talkie."

Without more, the two men soared past the active supply lines and found an outside stairway that was somewhat away from the treacherous hot spots. Speaking in his open monitor, Captain Williams said, "Chief, maybe this will give us some answers. Looks like the big heat is in front of you, Sir. Todd has a line that we grabbed. Have Mathew to tie it in at the foot of the stairs. Once it's set we're going on the roof. Looks alright!"

"That's too risky. It's an old building!" reminded the Chief, "Stay off the roof!"

"Has to be done, if the fire moves southward the whole town might blow! Half of the roof is gone; we can see down there! It's one pit from hell! Chief, here comes more trucks. Bring in that aerial rig from Buford to the south."

A voice came over the restored system, "We need to move some of these trucks... the paint is bubbling on #34."

A man cried out, "Somebody! Over here...I can't breathe!"

Captain could see a firefighter rush to his aid along with a standby emergency unit.

Another firefighter warned, "Move back! Move back! My God that wall is going to go! Get outta here!"

Meanwhile, Captain Williams and Fireman Todd moved onto the heated roof. They were well trained in this procedure. Williams stepped carefully on the rusted side-panel then quickly eased his footing onto a girder with several cross members. Any freeze had been melted by the heat. About forty feet below him was the smoldering pit that created plumes of rolling smoke against a red sky ablaze from the buildings and lumber.

Suddenly, Todd stepped forward onto a side section. There was an eerie snap and a snarl. He felt his foothold coming loose.

"Captain!" He screamed desperately while grasping for something to hang onto. "Oh, God! Please help me!"

Knowing the sound, the plea and the circumstances, Williams feared the worse. Instinctively, he hooked his rope to the girder and grabbed the flying man. He snatched him by the coat by pure luck.

"Todd, hold still, please be calm Hey, look up. We can do this! That's it!"

Below the fire pit was now slapping flames as if ready to swallow them both. Captain called out, "Slowly, take my wrist! Slowly! My wrist!"

The man was dangling yet with a very slight toe hold on a metal cross-piece. The slightest slip and he would be gone. The coat was not a safe hold. Will coaxed, "Come on... easy... get my wrist!"

Finally, the young firefighter grasp Will's wrist and Todd grasp his for a double hold. Todd's foothold suddenly snapped away and dropped below into the flames. His life was now in the hands of Williams.

On the ground, the Chief was hearing the episode on the roof through the open mike. He rushed several men to assist. He was hearing Captain Williams plead, "Hold on Todd! I've got you! My rope is secure!"

Williams was actually praying his rope was truly secure or they'd both be goners. Other firefighters were already dragging the dead weight of their water line getting it out or the way.

While two others reached the top to see Williams holding onto Todd, they started to rush to them. Williams yelled, "Don't come too close. Get me another rope. Pitch it in front of me!"

A firefighter obeyed. His first throw connected to a spot where Captain could use it. "Todd, I'm pushing this rope down... take it easy; get it with your other hand! Easy, do it easy. Get a good hold. That's it!"

Once Todd hooked onto the looped end before him, he clung with a steady grip. Williams nodded to the rescuing firefighters to tighten the rope and slowly pull him to a spot where Williams could help him to safety.

"Get out of here!" Williams screamed and pushed Todd to the metal stairway. They ran part way down the steps then jumped clear onto a pile of sawdust.

A loud boom on the underside brought the rest of the roof crashing down. Thick smoke spiraled upward. Snapping violent flames rekindled.

The sky was as if the whole world was aflame from the shooting embers and hungry flames.

The firefighters were weary and grateful for the many neighboring fire companies who had met the call with equipment and manpower. Every line was combating the brutal outraging beast that seemed to want to swallow the whole town. With deep anxiety, fear and anticipation, each firefighter began to slowly win with his part to slay the dragon. As one group, they brought it under control... now it would be to maintain.

Adrenalin flowed as the hours played the waiting game on through the night and into the next morning, the next day and until it would be totally over. There would be more days for continual watch for hot spots that could rekindle. Units and crews would be on constant alert.

Capt. Williams and Todd sat at the long table in the firehouse mess hall. Both had received cuts and bums from their narrow escape. Their heroic deed to get above the fire played a major role in saving the city. They were able to disperse information that was vital to conquer the mass destruction. Weather, wind and truck accident added to the difficulty. As they say afterwards, "It could have been worse if"

RECIPES FROM THE FIREHOUSE

BEST EVER POUND CAKE

3 1/2 Sticks Butter (Room Temp.)
1 Pkg. Cream Cheese (8 oz.)
Blend together in mixer (Slowest speed) until creamy, about 5 min.)
Add and blend at slowest speed for about 10 minutes. Let stand 15 minutes.
½ teaspoon Salt
3 ¼ Cups Granulated Sugar
1/3 cup very hot water

Add:
7 Eggs, X-Large (Wash eggs. Check each egg by placing in cup one at a time and check for spots or any undesirable odor that should be thrown out. Pour into butter mixture each good egg and blend to disappear.
Add: (1/3 amount at a time) Place all flour together, mix slow until each amount disappears.
2 ½ cups Plain flour (White Lily)
½ Cup Self-Rising Flour
1/8 teaspoon Baking Powder

When adding flour, after second amount of flour, pour in& mix. Then mix rest in.

1 Teaspoon Vanilla Flavoring
1 Teaspoon Almond Flavoring
Let stand to blend (5 to 10 min.)

Have Angel Food cake pan lightly greased with Crisco (snout too) Make a pan collar (due to the fact this cake rises extra high), Cut Strips of Wax paper about four inches across paper width fold in half and grease slightly. Put around the top edge of pan and grease lightly, this will extend outside height.

Flour lightly and shake any excess. Pour batter evenly in pan.

Place in ready 340-degree oven.

Bake for 1 hour and 23 minutes. Don't open oven while baking, it could cause the cake to fall. When done, remove and put onto cake plate (while hot) Cover tightly with pot and let cool.

Keep in air-tight container. Serve. This is great to freeze by slice or parts!

CHAPTER TWO

A news team was interviewing Commander Bailey for the 6:00 news. He had a make-up artist to give a makeover and was wearing his dress uniform for his politically correct interview regarding White Lumber fire.

Todd whispered to Williams, "Don't he look 'pertly'? Hope they don't sniff his breath!"

"Sssssssh," Smiled Will. "Hush!"

"We're at Old Town's Fire House #1. Let me introduce Commander Bailey who is the man in charge here. He's the hero of this last tragic fire at White Lumber Company, a major contributor of this city. Hello Commander Bailey"

"Hello Brad."

"Tell us what you did to save the city from total disaster."

"Well, uh, Brad, uh, I, uh, uh... I had my crews ready as always. We received the call and at first bell we were there. Timing is everything!"

"You were giving the commands, in charge of it all?"

"Sure, that's my job!" Bailey smiled widely as he told his 'white fabrication'.

"Single handedly, you directed this fire of the century. Wasn't the weather a real deterrent?"

"Not really. Once the equipment and men are in place, the heat will make it like Florida?" He snickered thinking he had spoken so brilliantly. "I'm used to fire calls!"

"What about the two fire trucks that wrecked on the way to the scene?"

"Oh that? We're still investigating why those trucks weren't tire chained. Uh, that, uh... uh is the fireman's job. We didn't have had enough time before the fire. Uh... I will personally check into that. We did have our neighboring fire departments come to our aid and help where needed." Bailey cleared his throat.

"Were there any life threatening happenings?" continued Brad.

"Nothing spectacular... just a big building and business burned to the ground. Firefighters expect small bumps, bruises and bums. We fight fires not die for the event. Usually, insurance can upgrade a situation. The fire is still under investigation, uh... but that's routine."

The interview continued.

Todd whispered, "That nut! Did you hear that? He makes me sick! He wasn't even at the scene! The Chief and you ran the show! The jerk was probably drunk if we knew the facts! Humph! Everything was at risk! I could be dead and you too!"

Todd became louder. Williams gave him the look and whispered, "Shhhhh!"

It became too much for Todd. He yelled out, "If it weren't for Capt. Williams I'd be dead now! Ask Bailey where he really was and what he did!"

They had just gone into commercial. The camera man yelled, "Cut! Hey buddy you have to keep quiet this is live. Thank God we're off camera!"

Captain Williams gave Todd a grunt as the Fire Chief joined them. He said, "What's important, we know the way it was and is. We're the real firefighters. Our world is 'The Call', Bailey is only a mouth piece. Nobody ever knows the whole facts. It's alright!"

"I suppose, but you are my un-sung hero!" said Todd as tears fell from his eyes.

The muscular Dalmatian stuck his nose into the crack of the door opening. Eyes shifted watching him wiggle in. Their mascot had special rights it seemed. The animal was smart and well mannered. He sat in front of Chief Thomas. With a slight whine, he held his paw to shake hands. The head firefighter obliged and said, "Sit!"

Immediately Mac plopped his rear to the floor and stared.

"What's his problem?" asked Brad "Guess he wants to be on television.

After all he's a greater hero than that 'mutt' over there," Todd grinned pointing at Bailey.

Noticing the dog with intrigue, the newscaster, Brad, moved to the small group. He asked, "Who is this?"

"He's our better half," laughed Thomas. "He's a character. Captain Williams here is his partner."

"Partner?" stammered William, "Sure he sleeps in your room and rides your truck."

He took his hat and put it on the dog's head and snapped his fingers, "Stay! Good Boy!"

"That's fantastic!" gleed Brad. "What more does he do? This is another story itself!"

"He has a job too. Mac, that's his name, watches over the equipment and trucks at fires."

"Wow! How about you and Mac come over here and let's finish our story with him?"

"Well I don't know... "

"Go on! Do the rest of interview," Said Chief.

Without words Commander Bailey was set aside with the replacement of a dog and his master.

Bailey was irate, "Sons-of-bitches! No class sons-of-bitches! I ain't finished yet."

"You're right, Mac really is a son of a bitch! But I don't think Captains mom is a dog, or a bitch!" grinned Todd enjoying getting even with Bailey.

The television crew completed their story and were hurrying to depart for their next assignment. Bailey kept talking to them. "Do you reckon I can get a copy of our interview? You know, the department needs to keep this kind of data."

Continuing to pack, the cameraman grunted. "This was live. They may have it at the studio. You can call them."

"Call them, he'll tell them to send it here!" he insisted.

"Look, we have to leave now...."

"Send that tape!" argued Bailey.

"I'll tell them!" the man snapped his camera case of extras together and rushed toward the door motioning his partner to come on.

The announcer laughed as he made long steps to catch up. "That fellow Bailey is something else. I believe we got the story from the wrong source."

RECIPES FROM THE FIREHOUSE

STRAWBERRY PRESERVES

2qt. Strawberries, sliced juice of 1-½ lemons
7c. Sugar
1 Tbsp. Margarine

Pour strawberries into a heavy pot. Add sugar to berries, stirring well. Let stand for 30 minutes. Separate berries from juice by straining. Blend berries for about 5 seconds, keeping course.

Pour berries and juice back into pot and stir well while bringing to a boil. Add lemon juice. Cook over medium heat for 1 ½ to 2 hours from boiling point. Add margarine; stir. Pour into jars and seal.

*For an unusual flavor add:
½ pkg. Frozen coconut add 1 tsp. Almond flavoring to ¼ of pureed mixture. Stir well; cook for 15 to 20 minutes. Put into jars and seal.

BLUE RIBBON FIG PRESERVES

10lb. Figs, halved
½ c. water
5-½ lb. Sugar

Combine figs, sugar and water. Let stand overnight (or 18 hours). Next day bring to a boil; reduce heat and cook for 2 ½ hours, stirring occasionally being careful not to let stick. Pack in jars and seal.

YEAST ROLLS

1c. med warm water
1 tsp. salt
2 pkg. yeast (114oz)
4 c. plain flour
1/3 c. sugar
1/3 c. Crisco shortening softened

In warm, thick and large bowl, place water. Sprinkle yeast in. Stir until dissolved.

Stir in salt and sugar. Use dough hook and add in flour until mixed well and forms into a good mix.

Turn onto a bed of flour and knead for about 7 minutes or until a smooth ball.

Place into a very large bowl that is heavily greased with Crisco. Cover dough with a coating of Crisco. Cover and place in warm place for about 1 to 1-½ hours or until dough is about double or more in size.

Punch dough down

(You can roll it if you wish.) Form a ball again.

On a floured surface knead dough until dough forms a nice ball. Throw it in the air and let it flop onto the counter.

Usually take it about three feet over head and throw it down on the counter about four times. This gets the bubbles out and makes a softer outcome.

Then again, form into a ball and roll it out into a square-ish flat, ¼» (pizza-like) crust. Pour 1 stick of melted butter over this and spread evenly, leaving about one inch without butter at the far side of the dough.

Grease your fingers and roll dough gently into a long roll. Stretch somewhat so it will make more rolls. Let rest about eight minutes while you grease liberally muffin tins with Crisco. Cut rolls in 1 ½ inch pieces and place (cut side or) flat side down in each tin cup.

Yield: 2 dozen rolls.

Again, let rise to double. Bake in 485-degree oven for 6 to 8 minutes or until golden brown. Brush with butter in pan then pour onto clean towel to cool slightly.

Cover in bowl with towel. Enjoy!

These freeze well and can warm in microwave for seconds.

CHAPTER THREE

C ommander Bailey strolled into the station as usual. His shift of twenty-four hours had started thirty minutes prior to his arrival. Todd was reading the newspaper with his morning coffee; others were in their sleeping quarters.

"Good morning Commander," he smiled.

"Good? What's so good?" growled the gray haired man.

"It's a beautiful day, nippy through."

"Hmph, ain't no different than yesterday. That today's paper?"

"Sure is, would you like to read it? I picked it up on my way in," Todd felt he had to justify his ownership of the twelve pages.

"Give me that second part," Bailey opened it quickly, "Yeah, March 12, 1991. Look at this!"

Todd glanced at a picture of a bride." Someone you know?"

"Of course, stupid! It's my ex-wife. Look at the fool. I knew she was ripping with that crazy old man. He owns the shoe repair on Tennis Street. I'll repair his ass one of these days!" Promised Bailey.

The Commander leaned over casting the picture fully in front of the young firefighter. Todd could smell the alcohol on his breath. He realized his uniform wasn't the usual starch-pressed-clean that was expected of city employees. Instead, it actually looked like he had slept in it. At the bottom of the pants was an unstitched seam. The other leg was wet maybe even vomit. A close look and there was a big gash over his nose that someone attempted to cover up with makeup.

"Commander, do you feel alright? You seem upset with this news. Captain Williams is here. You should go home," Todd suggested.

"You and Williams would like that, wouldn't you? I believe you're two 'perty boys' you hang so tight!"

Todd gritted his teeth. He stood, gathered his newspaper and walked out. The door accidentally slammed behind him.

Quickly Bailey jerked it open, and screamed, "Hey get back in here! You can't walk out on me. I'm your supervisor! Your superior!"

Todd stopped and turned, "Yes, Sir!"

"You're all a bunch of back stabbing devils. You want to get me fired. I see it and I hear you snicker behind my back. Get out there and tell the other six wack-o's to get to the command table right now!"

His eyes were red and seemed to water. Todd knew the "mood" was mounting to spite work. He exited to find the rest of the crew.

"Hey! Get into the kitchen Bailey is on his high horse!"

"Oh gosh!" moaned Della, "I saw his ex-wife's picture. I'll bet that's what roasted his goose."

"Oh yeah, it's well done now and smoking. You'd better hurry!" Todd's voice trembled. He was afraid of Bailey.

"Tell him I'm on the phone with the Chief," winked Captain Williams. "I'll be in after the flames die down."

The rest of the crew found chairs quickly at the long table in the kitchen that was a conference table when they needed it. They sat, waiting.

From down the hall they could hear the shuffling of Bailey's feet. He entered, and slammed a stack of papers on the table. Bailey turned to the coffee pot and poured himself a cup adding six sugar packs. The lights flickered with a snap of lightening and a clap of thunder.

"Who did that?" murmured the Commander.

"God I recon." Guessed a new firefighter.

"No kidding, I thought you did it!" growled Bailey.

"There's been enough game playing! Here are some new brushes. This place is a mess. I want this kitchen and the head spotless before five o'clock or you don't get supper!"

The crew stared at the brushes.

"Tooth brushes? How do you expect us to get anything done with these?" Todd questioned.

"If you'd do it right in the first place, you wouldn't have to scrub it now. Go on and get your buckets and scrub. I don't want to hear a word from any of you. Todd, when it's done, you can polish and buff."

He walked out. Soon they heard his room door slam.

"He's a spiteful jackass." Laughed Williams when he entered. He was mocking Bailey, enacting his gait, "Now scrub, I don't want to hear a word!"

"Never!" smiled Della, throwing a toothbrush to the Captain. She teased back, "Git your toothbrush! On your knees! See that crack there? Scrub, Buster, scrub!"

Someone turned the radio up. They commenced scrubbing and singing to the music. On the serious side of things, they all knew to do as told or the Commander would make life a greater hell. He loved to being a jerk.

Williams went to a storage closet and returned with a mop and bucket. He was starting to fill it when Bailey returned.

"Where's my orange ashtray?" He sputtered. "Todd? You ass, I know you have it! You are a sneaky slime! You'd better find it quick!"

"I don't know where it is!"

"You hid it! Ten bucks says you hid it!" he fumed. "I know you!"

The chief was standing at the door. They looked up in dismay. Being on their knees was now ridiculous and unexplainable. The Fire Chief wanted to laugh but kept a straight face. He knew this was more of the Commanders antics. He grinned, "Are you folks sick? Since when do you brush your teeth on your knees?"

Nobody dared to answer.

Bailey was in the hot seat. He turned bright red with embarrassment, "Uh-uh, they haven't cleaned this place in weeks! I figured I would emphasize the importance of cleaning. You know the City Council is going to visit here soon."

Chief Thomas said sternly, "Go to my office Bailey. You people get back to whatever you should be doing. There is no time for his childish games. If he ever plays games like this again, I expect you to call me. This is no place for such!"

Bailey had walked out and the Chief followed him to his office. Voices were muffled but it was the Chief doing most of the speaking. He was a good fair man toward his whole department. It was rare that he ever disciplined anyone. This was a newfound problem although he had heard rumors that Commander Bailey was acting out his misery.

After the confrontation, Bailey stomped out and rushed to his own office. His anger mounted. He took his arm and cleared his desk by sweeping everything to the floor. The breakage of various things sounded throughout the department.

He muttered to himself loudly, "Bastards! They will all pay some day. Yelp, they are a bunch of cotton pants! Petted little devils! Tattle tales!"

Once the drama was over, Bailey began to put his desk back together. As he was going through the mess he chuckled to himself, "Oh my Lord! Here's my orange ashtray! Damn, I'll have to glue the eagle back on!"

RECIPES FROM THE FIRE HOUSE

CHERRY CRUNCH SPECIAL

2 Large Cans Cherry Pie Filling
1 large Can Pineapple
¾ cup Sugar (granulated)
1 Box pineapple cake mix
2 sticks (melted) Butter
2 Cups chopped Pecans
Layer above items evenly into a greased long baking dish.
Place in 350-degree oven and bake about 35 to 45 minutes. Dip from dish.

LAYERED DESERT

1 Pkg. Cake mix (make to recipe, using one pan.
1 large Can Chocolate Pie Filling
1 Large Can Cherry Pie Filling
I Large Pkg. Frozen Coconut Huge Pkg. Cool whip (Plus)

Cut cake into large pieces and layer other items as desired over it in big bowl.

If desired, cover with added Cool whip and top with ½ cup chopped nuts

CHAPTER FOUR

The crew had completed paper work and getting the kitchen back to normal. The wife of a visiting firefighter slipped into the side door with a huge pot and placed it on the stove. She grabbed the big potholders and blew at her fingers, "That is still boiling hot! Thought you might like a good lunch. It's not much, brats and kraut. Hope you'll enjoy! There's bread in the car and that Grape Dessert that Robert loves. I'll be right back."

Chief Thomas put his stack of work down and smiled. "Come on and join us. I can't think of anything better!"

Della joined in, "Oh great, I love Brats. Let me help you. We'll keep you hostage until all the food is inside."

Everything was finally in place and everyone was at the table with their first plate. Todd licked his lips. "This is the kind of woman I'm looking for! What a cook!"

Della winked, "You're right, she is a keeper!"

A few bites and the big horn screamed its call for duty. The fire crew quickly jumped from the table leaving everything and ran for their station. Turnout gear was in place by the trucks. They struggled into it and rushed into their place on their truck. The engines started, lights were flashing and the bay doors were sliding up. All was set.

Todd was driving for Captain Williams for the first time. He nervously asked, "Now? Drive out now?"

Williams patiently nodded to go. He reminded him, "Hit the siren and drive careful. Don't take any chances."

A few vehicles were randomly around the road. It made it difficult to get through. It is one thing to practice driving a fire truck but another to

26

take it out for the real thing. Williams urged, "They're stopped! Go on! That's it, you are doing great!"

The truck seemed fast because of the loud sirens and deep horn. Immediately Todd was comfortable with his task and it all fell into routine. He listened for orders for the location of the fire then rolled through the streets to the designated place.

Todd brought the big rig to the best location for the event. A fire hydrant was very conveniently located in front of the place. They could see what had to be done and raced to put lines into place and start the battle against the devil. The small frame house was engulfed. Expertly the firefighters were under the lashing flames. They were knocking it down and smoke was bellowing.

A man rushed screaming toward the truck. He cried, "Please! My son is inside! Please! Help us!

Although the fire was getting under control this new problem was devastating. A human life was at stake.

"I'm going in!" shouted Della.

"I'm behind you!" determined Todd.

"Go!" ordered Williams. He watched the two make their plan on their way through the front door.

The two knew the danger for themselves. As they entered the first room they could feel the heat and were aware debris was falling around. They both had only the light from their flashlights in the total dark created by the power having been cut and the smoke.

"It didn't take long to get charred, it sure is black!" Della spoke. "Lots of smoke."

They both activated their oxygen supply. Todd quickly reported the circumstance to the Captain through his communications system. "See if the informant can give us a clue where the son is. We can barely see in here."

The best of firefighters must keep their perspective and not lose their way. It is easy to get turned around with the darkness and new circumstances.

Della was shining her dim light toward another doorway and tripped. Instantly, she fell to the floor.

Retrieving her composure, she began feeling around, "Todd, it's the victim. Over here, I tripped on his leg. Come get him!"

"I'll take him out! Shine the light on the exit door."

They heard the boy whimper when Della pushed the boy into the arms of her partner. Another firefighter rushed in to replace Todd.

Outside medics placed the child on a waiting gurney and began assessing him for damage. He was scared but alive and unharmed.

Della was still on the floor. Her heavy turnout gear made it difficult to stand up. Strangely though, she thought she heard movement. She began crawling on the floor in its direction. Even with gloved hands she thought she felt a human limb. "Hey, there is somebody else in here!" She choked.

Todd had returned inside the house. "Della?"

"There is somebody else right here! I feel something. Yes, I feel a leg."

She kept patting the area and found a kitchen type table was sheltering the body. "Bring your lights," She ordered her buddies. Both of the men were at her side trying to put things in order. Then, they heard a moan, then a cough.

"Can you hear me?" barked Blake, the other firefighter. He had adjusted his gear to better observe and continue the body search. "She's under the table."

Todd and Blake joined Della to free the woman from her plight. "Turn the table on its side." Suggested Blake. Once they had full access to the person, they each knew she probably needed oxygen.

"Hey, lady we have to get you out of here. This smoke is severe! Can you understand?" Todd urged. "Can you hear me?"

He quickly gave her a shot of his oxygen. She was a big woman, "She's heavy! Give me a hand Blake."

The dead weight was difficult. However, the two men tried to hoist her out. Finally, the woman grunted.

"Thank God! Can you understand? We are in your house and it has burned with fire. Do you understand?"

They kept moving her to the doorway. Once there, other crew joined them to retrieve the woman. As she was being removed from the building, they could hear her start to struggle to come alive. Blake saw her eyes flicker, "Put her down! Get the medics!"

"Where's Della?" Todd cried. "We'd better get her!"

With the woman out of their hands both firefighters rushed back to find their partner. With better light they could see Della half on the floor by the table. She puffed, "I can't take any more. Get me out of here!"

Della was dazed from the heat and was overwhelmed with the search mode. Her oxygen was in place but not turned on. Quickly Todd flipped a button and it began proper operation. "Can you walk?"

She nodded yes and leaned on him as they forced their way out.

"What happened?" Captain inquired.

"That woman needed help. We thought she was dead. Della used her own lifeline on her. The heat, smoke and toxins in there were absolutely overwhelming." Supplied Todd. He took her helmet off.

"Get her to the hospital!" demanded Williams.

Della began to return to normal and sat up, "I'll be fine!" She took some deep breaths and smiled. "See, I'm perfect."

Todd had to tease when he realized his partner was safe. "Hot dog, now is my chance! Let me take her out of her clothes!"

Even though Della seemed recovered, Captain insisted that she ride the EMC Unit to the hospital. "We had better play it safe, besides she might eat all our brats if we let her go back to the station before us."

Williams and his crew kept working the fire. They wanted to determine the specific cause if possible and be certain all hot spots were controlled.

Once more, there was a call from the station announcing another CALL. This one was about six blocks from this fire.

The Captain listened intently on the radio, "Engine 29 are you about to leave your post?'

"No, we are still involved. It will take time to finish here. We had two people to rescue and the house is a complete loss and is still a hazard. We cannot leave." Insisted Captain Williams. He listened for the next direction.

The radio rattled with static and was echoing the sound of engine horns. "Engine Four, go on to Baker Street. It is reported a fire on a lot.

They said the owner is burning trash and needs help." The dispatcher cleared his throat.

"Captain Williams what is your situation regarding time?"

"We will be here several more hours. We sent Della to the hospital with the child and lady that were rescued out of that house. They will all recover. They suffered smoke inhalation and needed oxygen."

"Keep us posted! Engine twelve is at the other location now. We will send you more men if you need." Dispatcher suggested.

"Good, send the Chief here. A newspaper reporter has arrived. He can wait for his news," Added the Captain. "Oh my night! Here comes Blake with a big old dog in his arms. My, my! It looks like Fido is dead!"

"Captain," cried Blake, "Help me start CPR here!"

Another firefighter helped lay the beast on the ground so they could start rescue. Blake pushed on the animals' chest and counted, then held his snout and blew air. He repeated the procedure several times and the dog opened his eyes and began to wiggle. He wanted to get up but they forced him to stay. Blake gave it oxygen from his supply then let it loose. She scampered away in fear and confusion.

"You got her! She's alive!" screamed a neighbor. "How terrific! Come here Ruby! Come here!" The dog rushed to the crying woman and flipped into her arms.

An hour went by before the dispatcher was announcing another CALL. You could hear the loud background noise at the headquarters station house.

Three CALLS in a short period of time and lunch was still sitting on the table at the station. Williams was listening to the dispatch while analyzing his current situation. The house was now contained. Everyone was somehow safe and Blake had administered 'mouth to snout' on Ruby. He knew the small truck could retain security at this residence and complete this part of the mission.

Once the address was delivered, Williams acknowledged, "Alright, we're ready. Just one line left to put back on the truck!"

"Captain, that's great." Continued the Dispatcher. "You're going to a huge situation on the entrance pocket at the Interstate."

"Yes, I heard. A melting crew will stay here. The Chief will stay. We are on the way!" replied Williams. "You said a semi-truck and trailer overturned?"

"Right, and a pile-up of other vehicles! Get out there!"

The Fire Chief took over the house fire with the staying crew. He had heard the radio and knew Engine 27 had to roll. The blasting horns and screaming siren opened the way for Todd to manipulate the vehicle to reach the next CALL.

RECIPES FROM THE FIREHOUSE

MANHATTAN CLAM CHOWDER

2 cans Baby Clams

2/3 Stick Butter

Teaspoon Black Pepper & salt to taste Place in large Soup pot. Gently braise for about 12 minutes on medium low heat.

2 Cans Evaporated Milk (plus 2 cans water) Pour into Clam pot bring to simmer.

Add ½ Cup or more Tomato Ketchup Stirring together slowly to blend.

Have ready: 3 cups boiled diced potatoes and 1 chopped onion. Add to Clam pot after Ketchup.

Bring all together to a smooth simmer and heat to near boil. Add salt if needed.

Serve in bowls with bread or crackers. Top with fresh parsley for a neat decoration.

Serve as a meal or cup-of with meal.

CHAPTER FIVE

"I'm starving!" Groaned Captain Williams. "I'll try to get our brats sent over if it looks like we'll be there a while. I get weak if I don't eat. We need food."

Captain flipped a switch and reached the kitchen at the station. "Is Blakes' wife still there?"

A voice answered, "Yes, she's already fixed the food into sandwiches. We have it on the way to you now. We know you'd eat a door off the truck if you can't get food! Can you believe Commander Bailey ordered us to do this? He might be human after all!"

"Thanks! I see the car now. If we don't eat, we can't keep on. Some of us might have had a bite." He complained. "Oh boy! We have a real mess here! I see the semi and its trailer. There's white stuff everywhere!"

Their dog Mac, jumped from the truck as soon as it stopped. The food supply was brought to them and they snapped it up quickly. Mac wasn't bashful about retrieving his share.

Todd informed, "Great! Captain Bo Johnson is in command. We're the second truck here. We need to know what the truck was hauling."

The late lunch that turned out to be dinner bridged the hunger and made continuing possible. Captain Williams rushed to Captain Johnson, "What is all that white stuff out there. Here comes the snorkel! What a real mess!"

"Right! Glad you're here. Don't get too close. A big eighteen wheeler that has just over turned is very unpredictable. In fact, it could even blow!" Winced Johnson. He was directing the situation. "See this? Just look at it! Chickens are all over the place! Chickens, alive and dead, are in cages and walking around. We still can't find the truck driver. We must make certain this cab doesn't catch fire. We need to contain the structures. Look under there, that's a little car. See it? What do you think we need to do?"

"Did they order heavy rescue? They should already be here!" proclaimed Williams.

"Rescue always comes to this type of CALL. I don't know what is taking so long! We need that rig off that little Ford."

Early evening was quite dark. This emphasized the crimson lights of the oncoming rescue crews. Traffic was totally shut down on the North side of the four-lane interstate that was divided with a curtain of evergreen trees.

A man dressed in white pushed by them, along with two others carrying a portable stretcher. He yelled, "Where are the victims?"

"We just got here! We don't know!" answered Captain Johnson.

"What's wrong with you people? Are you too stupid to search?" The medic challenged. "We're ready for transport!"

"Everybody is already searching. We have just arrived ourselves!" Williams injected.

"Yeah? What about the food in your mouth?" He judged.

"We've been all day at a fire call and had our lunch sent here. My men have to eat. Did you eat today? We can't go on without food." Explained Captain Williams. He was exhausted from the last CALL and nerves on edge. "Maybe you need a big boot up your ass!"

"Bring it on, Mr. God!" The man growled with a fist drawn.

Quickly Todd jumped between the men, followed by Captain Johnson. "Hey, this is not the place! Will, go over to the big wrecker that just pulled in and direct that."

From what seemed 'out of nowhere' Mac flew through the air and knocked the man in white to the ground. Quickly he held him firmly at the neck with his mouth. Saliva dripped and his eyes sparkled waiting for a command.

The whole crew wanted to laugh. Todd snapped his fingers and demanded, "Mac, stop! Come!"

Proudly the big spotted fire dog released his subject and rushed to Todd. "We have a job to do. This is finished." Ordered Captain Johnson.

Williams rushed to the wrecker that was stopped for instructions. Mac joined his favorite buddy. He gave a low growl and motioned with a flip of his head. Quickly he grabbed Captain's hand, pulling hard and whining.

"Alright boy, go!" Ordered Williams.

The dog rushed off and looked back to be certain he was being followed. He loved the challenge of rescue. With several leaps he charged through a hole below the drive wheel of the rig's cab. The little beast disappeared by sliding in the space. Nothing moved.

Concerned, Williams called, "Hey, Mac, Mac!"

He responded with a bark to inform them he was okay. The sound of a man swearing overrode all other noise. "Oh God! A dog," The voice expelled. "Help! Please! I can't move! There's a dog here! Help!"

Mac was ordered out of the hole. Williams reached for a bottle of water and handed it to him. "Take it to him. Go, Mac!"

Obediently, he snapped it up and happily rushed to take the water to the victim. They heard movement and ordered the dog out. Williams knew it was vital to get the big rescue unit in place quickly. They could not try to reach the driver until the rig was stable. "Mister, try to hold on. We have help right here. Can you hear me?"

"Yes, will you get me out? I can't move. I'm trapped here!" Driver seemed to be suffering. The man inside began to scream hysterically.

"You're going to be okay! Calm down!" She cautioned. "This has to be done. Cover your face!"

Mac wanted to jump free but was held by words. He whined and watched.

The smoke diminished and investigators determined the next stage of recovery. The driver was next priority. You could see the front end and roof of the car were demolished but the rest escaped major crushing. This should be at least a bit helpful. Although glass was everywhere, it was hard to know from which vehicle. It looked odd to see the rig and car entwined with each other waiting for escape from the scene.

Firefighter Gina Ballard dropped the extinguisher beside the road and cautiously moved toward the Ford. She knew someone was wedged there. The crews could hear him yell and puff.

She soothed, "Sir! You have to relax. The wreck is over! We need you to calm down so we can get you out of here! Tell me your name!"

"Hold on. We have the equipment here! They're working now! Just stay still."

The wreckers hooked lines to several parts of the big truck. They expertly tightened the thick cables. Signaling when to move, the rig was eased from the top of the car.

The mangled mass made a huge noise as the cables lifted and slid the rig to a safe spot. The car remained wedged in the deep hole of the ditch. There was no other way to rescue the driver. He was still out of sight.

Mac began to tug at Williams boots. He wanted to return to the driver. "Hold on! We have to appraise the situation. We'll get him!"

"That's weird! Looks like the car was hiding underneath!" Remarked Johnson. "Holy Mercy! It's on fire. See the smoke! Bring that great big extinguisher quick! It's smoking!"

In heavy fire turnout clothing a very small woman rushed to the situation. She snatched the pin and began easing toward the car spraying the smoke area.

"Bryan!" He responded in tearful fear. "Bryan Jones. Can you get me out soon? I hurt everywhere!"

"Yes, of course. Just tell me. Are you bleeding?"

"I recon so, there's blood everywhere," Bryan replied.

"That's to be expected with all the window breakage. Can you move?" She pressed.

The man tried to move his limbs and panicked again. "Oh gez! I can't move anything except my right arm! Help me! Please!"

"We're ready now!" She informed. "We have to cut the car to get you out. The big heavy rescue unit is in place. They are experts and will have you out soon. Do what they tell you, Bryan."

Two men in black coats with yellow stripes that reflected were discussing what to do next. "Cut here and here. These post should snap easily and we can pick the top off."

Quickly they followed their plan as they shouted details around as grinding began. All eyes were focused on the car now becoming a convertible. They pulled the top away exposing a shattered glass covered interior and a frightened man.

"He's still in his seat belt!" Gina Ballard rejoiced. "Our paramedics are here. We will help you out. Bryan, try to listen to them!"

They worked their way to the car. It was fully cradled in a big hole of a ditch and would not move. This would make rescue simpler. Getting Bryon on a backboard and a state of freedom was now happening.

"My car! It's ruined!" whimpered the nervous man.

"Let's think about you. A car can be replaced! Can you see my finger?" Quizzed the medic.

Immediately, he saw the man slip into a state of unconsciousness. "Come on! Move him! He has to get to the hospital now! He may be in shock. I can't do anything here! Go!"

It was quite a task to free Bryan Jones and ultimately have him on level ground. "I'm starting CPR; I'm not getting anything! Bryan, can you hear me?"

A partner handed the medic a mouthpiece. He positioned quickly and blew breath into the man's mouth. He counted and continued the procedure. Another medic was talking to the hospital explaining the circumstances. They continued as they talked on the direct communications device.

"He has a heart bracelet, look!" A medic discovered. "Get the defibrillator!"

It seemed his life was hanging by a thread. They worked desperately. "Clear!" The body seemed to jump. The EMT again called out, "Clear!"

This time he checked and located a heartbeat.

A gray helicopter hovered overhead and quickly settled on the closed traffic lane. The big cross on the side identified the machine from the nearby hospital. A door opened as a white coated man motioned clearance for them to bring the patient.

Automatically, the rescue team slid the patient through the opening into the receiving hands. Moving to clear, one medic stayed with the helicopter and provided information and paperwork. They were airborne in minutes.

On the ground, responders continued with their duties. It was shambles all over the road.

Mac quickly gave a big bark and jumped from his place beside the truck. Captain Williams let out his whistle command but the canine was on a mission. He disappeared into the tall heavy brush. In minutes they could hear his plea with a bark. The dog was calling the Captain for help.

Williams and Gina Ballard looked at each other. Captain ordered, "Come on, he's on a trail!"

Running in the direction of the bark, they parted the brush with their long flashlights and immediately found Mac. Gina glowed in awe, "My goodness! He has found somebody! Amazing! How could he know?"

The two dropped on the ground on each side of the man who was face down. Mac whimpered and pawed at the dirt. Captain quickly slipped off his gear gloves and slid on emergency rubber gloves. "Can you hear me?"

He rolled the man to his side and saw blood coming from his nose. "Ballard, Get help! Go! Hurry!"

Gina obeyed. She rushed away and found other firefighters who had followed. She breathed, "Come on! Hurry! It's a man! He's unconscious! We need EMT."

She led the group to Captain Williams and his victim. They could see him talking to the fellow.

"Buddy, you'll be alright. Help is here. I have to get back to the accident scene." He commanded. "Take over here!"

"I'll handle this, Captain," offered Jon Mayer. He was in a white uniform. His Red Cross patch on the arm of his shirt stood out over all the other patches. All emergency folks knew him for his abilities, officer in the Red Cross, registered nurse, and a number one paramedic.

He said, "Well done, Captain." He continued the revival. "So, Mac found you! You must be the driver from the truck. How did you get over here?"

The scared man replied, "I don't know!"

Returning to the main scene, Captain Williams could see the situation was well organized. Other wrecked vehicles were exiting the scene under their own power or being towed. Some of the emergency units were returning to their origination post.

"Mac!" whistled Williams. "Mac!"

Captain Bo Johnson scratched the edge of his head where perspiration was seeping from under his helmet, "This has been a crazy night, Williams. Sure glad they sent you with Mac. He's quite a fellow."

"Mac! Come on Buddy! Called the tired man. "Bo, we're all glad to be here! I just wonder what that Mac is doing. He always answers. Oh, well, he's probably tired and went to the truck. Do you know what actually happened here?"

"The highway patrol has been investigating the actual accident. There were six other vehicles involved besides the rig and that Ford. Sgt. Miller told us the Ford that was in the ditch came from the other side of the highway. He ran several others into each other. He was heading right straight into the big rig. The trucker tried to miss him but couldn't quite make it. The car ended up in the ditch and the rig on top of him. The shoulder gave way and flipped the trailer. He had thousands of chickens in little cages going to market."

"Man! Look at all the dead chickens and feathers!" amazed Williams.

"They've been picking up live birds for the last hour. The creatures are everywhere! The dumb-ox birds don't realize this is not the way to go to market!" smirked Johnson and pointed, "Is that Mac?"

"Oh no! It sure is! That nut has wet himself and rolled in all those loose feathers. Look at him! He's covered completely! Mac! Come here!"

The dog was panting hard while moving his small flock of chickens to the fire truck area. The group of white birds squawked and scampered accepting the canines' direction. They jumped, clucked and shook their feathers. Mac forced them into place beside a big ladder. He sat starring as they finally found a spot to roost on a fire hose.

"I'm not believing this!" laughed Williams. "Those chickens are so tired they are sleeping! Dig that!"

Bo Johnson was laughing so hard he doubled to the ground. "This is too much! Look at your dog! He looks like a four-legged turkey! Maybe he's really Big Bird!"

Surrounding officers and firefighters joined in the laughter and comments.

"Why don't you paint him Yellow?" crowed one.

"I have a better idea. He's so good at everything, why not paint him pink and he could deliver babies!" smiled the highway patrolman. "Be a good flamingo!"

"Are you nuts? A flamingo doesn't deliver babies, you dummy. Storks deliver babies!" crowed a medic.

"Sh-sh-sh!" Calmed Captain Williams. "Please don't give Mac any more ideas. He's listening to every word you're saying. Look at the poor tired boy! He's roosting with his chickens! Leave him alone, he's tired."

They watched him roll over on his back with his eyes shut and grinning.

Everyone smiled when the beast sighed deeply.

RECIPES FROM THE FIREHOUSE

GRAPE DESSERT

(Make a day before serving) Pick a large bunch of red or black grapes, be sure they are sweet and seedless. Remove stems, bad ones. Clean, dry, and place in large Oblong Pyrex dish (10x16x2) or such. Use glass not metal with cream deserts)

MIX TOGETHER: 8 oz. Package Cream Cheese (room temperature

8 oz. Sour Cream
1 teaspoon Vanilla
½ Cup Powdered Sugar

SPREAD OVER THE GRAPES.
IN A FRY PAN: TOAST 1 ½ CUPS PECANS IN ¾ STICK OF BUTTER. (Don't use margarine and don't use real high heat)

REMOVE FROM BURNER when toasted and add ½ cup light brown sugar. Stir and sprinkle over top of readied dish. COVER WITH PLASTIC WRAP.

REFRIGERATE UNTIL READY TO SERVE.

Cut into squares and serve. A very light but rich desert with a surprise when your guest discovers the grapes!

CRAB BOIL

Select the big Dungeness crab about 2 pounds or so per person. Clean shells.

Boil huge pot of water and add plenty of sea salt (or plain salt). Place crab into water and boil until crabs tum the beautiful red. Maybe 15 minute.

Remove from water onto a serving platter and let everyone go for it!

Guest should have heavy plate, fork, nut-crackers, skinny knife or prong, lots of napkins and maybe a bib!

Dip: Melt butter serve on the side. Some people like other sauces like cocktail or tarter. Crab is so sweet it needs very little help!

Let's keep the Crab Fishermen in Alaska in business!

RABBIT SOUP

1 Full saddle of a young rabbit
3 egg whites
3 ounces cream cheese (In one-inch cubes)
8 ounce can garden peas, drain well
2 cups chicken broth or can chicken broth
1 teaspoon dry sherry
1 Tablespoon cornstarch, (1/4 cup cold water) to mix at time of use.)
¼ cup milk
2 Tablespoons minced boiled ham (optional)

Cover rabbit with water in a large pot and boil until meat is tender and falling off the bones.

Remove from broth. Remove bones and discard. Set aside pot of broth.

Slice and mince rabbit meat.

Beat egg whites until stiff and mix with rabbit meat. Set aside.

Dissolve cornstarch in ¼ cup cold water.

In medium pot mix 2 cups rabbit broth Chicken broth, add salt and bring to boil

ADD: PEAS, MILK, CREAM CHEESE, SHERRY AND BOIL FOR TWO MORE MINUTES.

REDUCE HEAT ADD CORNSTARCHMIXTURE. Stir continuously until soup thickens.

RAISE HEAT, gently STIR IN RABBIT MEAT.

As soon as it boils, soup is ready. Sprinkle minced ham on top.

*NOTE: IF YOU DON'T HAVE A RABBIT, a chicken would do. Then again, you can substitute turkey for rabbit.

WHEN MAKING FOR A LARGE GROUP, TRIPLE RECIPE. Lots of people serve crackers or rolls with stews and soups. A salad is great. Chop mixed lettuce for number of guest. Add tomatoes, spring onions, dry cranberries, and pecans then toss to mix. Sprinkle a bit of salt, pepper and Raspberry Vinaigrette, toss lightly and serve in large bowl.

BRATS AND SAUERKRAUT

As per package of 8 to 10 Bratwurst. Use your favorite brand.

Boil Brats for 6 to 8 minutes, this freshens them.

½ pound Barrel Cured Sauerkraut (Comes in plastic pouch in deli at most grocery stores. NEVER USE CANNED KRAUT.)

Olive Oil

Horseradish Mustard

Mayonnaise (Real)

Small Chopped Onion

½ Cup Chopped Kosher Pickles (Your choice)

1 Cup grated mild Cheddar Cheese

1 Package Seeded Long Rolls or Loaf of Pepperoni Cheese Loaf (Round)

*TOAST BREAD LIGHTY IN OVEN.

PREHEAT OVEN TO 400 degrees

1. Use foil covered long baking sheet.
2. Place All toasted bread in pan.
3. Place BRATS (Split longwise if desired)
4. Lay Brats across bread using half of bread (every other one)
5. Spread Sauerkraut evenly on the other half of bread.
6. Smear Mustard and Mayo over Brats.
7. Sprinkle Onion and pickle over Kraut.
8. Shake Olive Oil onto open sandwiches.
9. Add Cheese over all.

Bake for 8 to15 minutes.

LET GUEST SERVE THEM SELVES.

NOTE: Make as a RUBIN. You can try with ham or any other cold cut, this works for that also. Enjoy!

CHAPTER SIX

"Where's my orange ash tray?" Screamed the red faced Commander Bailey. "That Todd's on shift, I know he's got to be the one! Boy, you'd better find it right now!"

At first glance, you could see drool slipping from the comers of his mouth. His uniform shirt was not white anymore as it should be. He was cross even with himself. Drinking seemed to have taken over his brain. Nearly everybody and everything posed some sort of a problem or threat to him.

Captain Williams intervened quickly, "Bailey, cool it! Look here, your orange ash tray is right here!"

"I'll swanny! Shore is," Bailey grinned sheepishly. "Well Todd likes to play tricks you know!"

'Maybe, but you need to get off his case. He does like you, we all do," Captain shifted his feet and winced. "The Chief wants you to come to his office."

"What does he need? It's eleven o'clock. I wanted to take the boys out to do inspections. We ain't been keeping that up." He boiled resentment.

"I'll get that underway for you. Go on and have your meeting with the Chief. I'll call the crew into the kitchen," assured Williams.

"Everybody wants to run the show! I can handle my own job, let it wait." He flipped. "I'll return in a few. That crowd never waits for my instructions. You get the picture?"

Bailey turned down the hall into Chief Thomas' simple office. He noticed a large vase of roses on the desk and several wrapped packages. "Looks like you you're having a party, Chief."

"We are, its Dellas' birthday tomorrow. My wife wanted to have a little 'to-do' for her today since she'll be off-shift on her big day. She's a real firefighter, totally dedicated. Missy feels sorry for her because she doesn't have a husband and she's turning twenty-eight." He noted.

"Humph! Twenty-eight? I never thought she needed a husband. She's always been one of us. You might say it's like she has ten or more husbands with all of us looking after her. That little tree there with little red bows, what's that about?"

"It's a money tree! My wife had the idea. She says a girl can always use money. We're supposed to pin bills to it."

"Good idea, here put this on it. Della might need a new pair of drawers. I try not to get into her business," Chuckled Bailey in a lighter mood. The fact Chief was his superior he would stay in check.

"Have a seat Bailey," offered Jerry Thomas in his official voice. "I need to discuss with you a serious situation."

Commander James Bailey took the suggested seat and waited. Finally, he said, "Okay, shoot."

"Alright, I won't beat around the bush. It's your drinking." Thomas searched his eyes for a sign of explosion. He had dreaded this conversation for quite some time. Besides being guilty, Bailey was on edge most of the time.

"Drinking? That, my friend, is my business. I ain't bothering anyone anyhow!" He growled.

"You may not think it isn't bothering anyone. It does. One thing for certain, you cannot drink on the job. That must be not be heard of; that our Commander is nipping on duty. Even the Mayor is onto this. He told me to bring you in for this conversation. You know the chain... The Mayor, City Council, Chief, Commander and on down." Related Thomas trying to be tactful and not rock the boat.

"The Mayor? That fake jackass? He drinks all the time. They have those high falutin' parties at the Country Club and big time it." James Bailey defended himself. "I've been there and seen it! Not only that he dances with the women like he's taking them home! The Mayor! Sh--!"

"Take it easy, James. This isn't about the Mayor. It's about your drinking on the job! That is what we have to address. It is a fact that booze impairs your thinking and ability to clearly make decisions."

Chief Thomas was trying to be diplomatic, but Bailey wanted to deny and be difficult. "Look, the crew and everybody else likes you but you are not the person you used to be. I know you've been tom up about your marriage break up. It happens to lots of people. Even so, this job requires 100% and nothing less. Booze, pills nor any false relief will solve anything. Maybe you need help."

The Commander jumped to his feet and glared across the desk at his boss, "Screw you, the Mayor and the whole crowd and the horses they rode in on and the dang horses' horse! You can all kiss my royal rear! Besides, I ain't drinking on the job. Somebody is a liar!"

"Commander, we know you are drinking on the job. Not one incident but many. Open your desk drawer and look in, it's there. In your car outside, it's there. In your bedroom, it's there. Wherever you are, there is a bottle."

Pointed out the Chief. "We all know. Listen! You don't have but a couple years until retirement. You have a lot of time with the city and you deserve your benefits. Just do the right thing or you can lose it all!"

Thomas spun around in his swivel desk chair. "Remember; there was a time that you wanted to be Fire Chief. Don't lose sight of your dreams. If you let yourself get fired, then your future here would really be history."

"Yeah, dreams! There ain't none!"

"Life is always good even when we don't think so. You have to get a grip. Maybe you should get a little help. Here, go see Doctor Benson. Maybe talking to him can be a beginning." Chief wrote on a sheet of paper and extended it to him.

Bailey stared at the paper and snapped it from his hand. "And if l don't want to?"

"You really don't have a choice. City Hall will accept this. Otherwise, they will take whatever steps they need to relieve you. Go see the doctor. You're a good man. You can fix this. We all want the best for you!"

Baileys eyes turned red, tears flowed. He felt powerless and humiliated. As he cried openly his broad shoulders shook. He pleaded, "Don't fire me! I ain't got nothing but my job!"

"Then see Benson, he can help you." Soothed Thomas. "If you are caught intoxicated on the job again, you will be fired instantly. Take today off and see Dr. Benson. We go back many years, I'm still your friend!"

Bailey rubbed his eyes on his sleeve and blubbered. "I didn't mean to do it here. It's just hard watching my old wife in the newspapers. I loved her Sometimes I get right stiff at night and when I come to work it hangs on."

"Well, Buddy, that's the rules for all of us, not just you. You're very different when you have that stuff in your system. Go ahead and take care of yourself." Encouraged Jerry Thomas. "The city has changed, you know. We have to work harder. There's more area and businesses and people. We need another station, trucks and personnel. It all keeps us on our toes. We need you! Now, go on! Get out of here before the horns blow!"

They stood and shook hands. Chief patted him on his back.

"I know you have to do what you have to do. I'll straighten up, I promise! See you tomorrow!"

Once Bailey departed, Chief Thomas requested Captain Williams to his office. He immediately came in and sat.

"Coffee?"

"Sure!" smiled Will. "Let me do the honors!"

"I have a cravat over there. I need a cup," grinned Thomas. "You know the City officials had a meeting about Bailey. They have received quite a few complaints about his behavior, you know, the booze. They appointed me to fire him!"

"No!" Williams gulped. "Oh my!"

"It took some doing but I talked Mayor into giving him one more chance. I reminded them he could retaliate and sue the town and win. You have to give notice of dismissal. Our contract says you have to give a long term employee warning with reason." Chief replied. "The Mayor told me that it's the talk of the town about his boozing."

"I expect it is. He smells like it most of the time. Then, his attitude is something else!"

"It's a fact, he's been half stoned for the last three months," Chief Thomas related. "I gave him warning. When he is here during your shift I expect you to report to me if he is hitting the bottle. This also goes for him coming in hung over. He cannot continue this behavior. If we over look this somebody else can do this too. There is a legal responsibility."

"Certainly. My crew just tolerates him. He's gotten so hateful and spiteful especially toward Firefighter Joe Todd. He looks for something to fuss about all the time. Nothing can please him and the men are treated like his personal servants. He's so paranoid since his wife left him. I have known that something had to give. He used to be great, a real congenial buddy. In fact, old Bailey was my boss when I first started out. He has changed." Discovered Williams. "I hope he can straighten up."

"An alcoholic lives a hard life. It's every bit as hard as a drug abuser. He denies it but he's in bad shape. Baileys voice has changed along with his attitude. To tell you the truth, if he doesn't accept real help soon, I'm afraid of what will happen to him. He is a real time bomb!" Worried the Chief. "No more bad behavior here. He'll be terminated on the spot! Have you seen him drink here?"

"He doesn't bring anything inside. Sometime ago I think some of the fellows saw him in his car taking a nip." Williams pondered. "He has really been wild at times. To avoid him was best."

"The rules will be posted. It will apply to all personnel and visitors. We are going to stop smoking too except in a designated area outside. It would be unreal to burn down the fire department with a cigarette. This is from the Mayor and City Counsel."

"I don't smoke so it doesn't affect me." Will shared.

"Right, neither do I. The rest of them will flip!" laughed the Chief. "This includes visitors especially."

"Do you know what the biggest catastrophe will be?" blurted out Williams.

They looked at each other, pounded palms and screamed together, "Where is my orange ash tray?"

The rest of the day was going well. Captain Williams and his crew covered a great deal of the city business area making inspections. Most business had fire alarms and extinguishers that were up to code. At times, someone might need a warning regarding out of date on an extinguishers charge. Then, drop cords often presented a situation that could be remedied on the spot.

As the day was ending, Della rushed back to the fire truck. She was almost out of breath and her big brown eyes were aflame. She panted, "Captain Williams, come here a minute! I have something to tell you!"

Her boss smiled, "What in the world has you so charged? It can't be that bad!"

She started whispering loudly, "The Pawn Shop... I was there checking things. It's crazy in there! That little pervert tried to grab my chest!"

Williams tried to hide a grin, "Well?"

"Well heck! I flipped out and knocked him on the floor!"

"Not so good! You need to be a bit understanding!"

"Yes, but he's still on the floor I guess." Della explained. "Maybe I killed him! He hit his head on some barbells. Not only that; when I looked into his back room behind those blue velvet curtains. I saw little bags containing some kind of white powder spread on a table."

"Oh boy, let's go back!" The Captain turned to Todd, "Call the EMT and Police. Tell them to meet us at the Pawn Shop! Hurry! Della may have killed him! I don't want that weasel to have a chance to change things. Every time we go there he sneaks around trying to hide his junk. He's a jackass!"

RECIPES FROM THE FIREHOUSE

CORNED BEEF/CHEESE POTATOES

Purchase a prepared corned beef from grocer. Be aware of weight Remove from plastic sleeve and place on rack in a big baking pan with a lid.

Pour cup of water in pan and place beef on the rack. Shake loosely the packet of seasoning over it. Sprinkle chopped onion over it. Drop pads of butter around top of it.

Preheat oven to 340 degrees. Place covered meat inside. Bake about 45 minutes per pound.

When done, pour off juices, remove to a platter and let rest 30 minutes. Slice across the grain.

Mashed potatoes: Boil 2 lbs. potatoes (peel and slice). When fully cooked, pour off water.

Stir in: 1 cup Sour cream, ½ stick butter, 2 teaspoons parsley, 1 Cup mild cheddar cheese and 3 slices American Cheese. Whip until light. Serve on top meat slices with butter garnish.

CHAPTER SEVEN

Immediately Della and Captain returned to the scene. A young helper was attending the shop. They walked past without words. A customer stepped in to look at a lawn mower beside the door.

In the back room, they found the owner still on the floor where he had dropped. Williams said, "Dang, don't say anything to anyone Della. This may be investigated. He's unconscious, not dead."

Della gazed in disbelief, "I just clobbered him under the chin with my fist! Just once! He slid several feet. I couldn't help it! The jerk grabbed my breast and I reacted. In fact, he pinched me hard! I didn't mean to half kill him!"

While they waited for emergency help, Captain took notes on the condition of the room. He counted about thirty-some bags of something. There was a great deal of jewelry on another table in a wad. The place was actually unclean with a single bed across the room. He surmised the sheets had never been changed but were well used.

They heard the man grunt. Captain whispered, "Della, look what you're missing!" He shifted his eyes toward the bed.

"Shut up!" she whimpered with fear. They were relieved to hear the sirens roaring their way toward the Pawn Shop. "Captain, did you check his pulse?"

"No. He's breathing fine. He isn't bleeding and he fell on his own stuff. You really needed to do nothing but call the EMT. It'll be alright."

They could hear a lawn mower inside the front of the store being started. It took a few pulls of a cord before it roared full blast. Soon the building was being filled with smoke and the terrible gas odor.

"They can't do that! It's dangerous!" Della coughed.

"Della, go to the truck. Get into your seat and wait! Send a couple men back here. Don't do anything else! Got it?" Ordered Williams hoping everything would solve itself without trouble. He certainly didn't want Della in a mess. He knew the facts would speak for themselves.

"Yes, Sir! I'm out of here!" She promised and clamored from the building to find refuge in her jump seat on the truck. She quickly made it appear that she was catching up their paper work. Still, her mind tried to relive the last half hour. Her thoughts kept buzzing the possibility that the old fool could die and she'd be in prison.

The Police vehicle and ambulance stopped in the middle of the street. As they dashed through the door, the customer with the lawn mower threw his hands in the air and cried, "I ain't done nothin'. He started the mower!"

The senior cop motioned for them to turn the equipment off. "The Fire Department called us. Where's Captain Williams?"

"I dunno!" panicked the man. "I'm just trying to buy this here mower."

"Don't leave. We may need to talk." The officer addressed the other man in the middle of the room. "And who are you?"

"I work here. I'm a salesman and in charge. Two other fire guys are in back there. They're doing inspections here. Nothing else is going on, just an inspection." He squawked and motioned.

The Policeman and his assistants gazed toward the curtained door pointed out from his finger. "Back here?"

The salesman shook his head. They caught his worried look and sweat on his brow. A large coke flipped onto the floor spewing its contents around. "Damn! I'll get killed for this."

The policeman ordered, "Stay out here, Joe. Don't let them leave and nobody in other than emergency personnel."

Grabbing the velvet curtains, the other two rushed through the entry. They were met with a man on the floor. Captain Williams was kneeling beside him. The man seemed lifeless.

EMT Robert Allen forged into the room, "What's up?"

"Looks like he fell. There's so much clutter I don't see how he could ever stand. We are doing fire inspections today."

"Did you check him?" Allen quizzed.

"I just got here. I started but there was nothing to do. He's breathing. We called you. Here, take over!" Williams removed himself abruptly. He definitely didn't want to tangle with the man's DNA.

Robert reached for the pulse and rolled his eye back. The man groaned, then, opened both eyes. He spits across the floor as he sat up. He shook his head from side to side and seemed to rattle.

Captain handed him a bottle of water from on a table. He grabbed it saying, "Where is that witch?"

Captain Williams felt totally relieved for Della. Then his disgust returned, "This is Police business now! Look over there."

"You can't snoop around here! I have my rights! Besides, that Fire woman about killed me. I'll sue the city for all its worth!" he ranted and rubbed his mouth. "Get a search warrant if you want to see something!"

"The fire department has a right to investigate these buildings. You have codes to maintain. Look at these raw wires on this lamp. Oh, yes, that fan over there is just twisted wire to wire. You've got quite a 'hot spot' here, ole boy. No! We don't need a warrant." Served the Captain.

The officer in charge requested additional police assistance. EMT Robert Allen continued to check the man for injury.

"Stop it! You stupid fool! I'm fine now. I fell on this thing. That woman pushed me... no, she slugged me for no reason. She'll pay for this." He resisted. Now look, my nose is bleeding. Just get outta here and leave me alone!"

Allen smiled, "He refused medical help and proclaims nothing is wrong with him. He's all yours. I'm gone!" He zipped his bag and motioned to his partner. The two left the room.

Williams stepped aside for the Police to begin their job. He took his clip board and scribbled quite a few notes that included many violations to city code. "You know you have to have a smoke detector in every room. There isn't one in here."

The Police walked around the room. They too noticed the unmade bed. "Do you live here?" One sarcastically grinned. "Where did you get this gun?"

"Hey, You scum-bag!" Screamed the pawnshop owner. "I told you, you ain't going through my stuff! I ain't got nothing to hide! I just don't want you jerking my things out of place! Quit it now! I take guns in on pawn. That's perfectly legal. I keep records on them."

"Relax, we are only checking behind Captain Williams and the fire crew. We are here to help. The Fire Department often calls us when there is an accident." The officer explained waiting for an opportunity to search. It didn't take long for the Police to discover the table with the packets of white and another door that was slightly open. The Police Sergeant exclaimed, "Well, well, well, well, well!"

"That's private there!" resisted the now pale-faced pawn owner. "I said get out!"

"What's this? Oh, I know. Powdered sugar, I'll bet! Is your mommy baking cakes today and you're making the icing?" Snickered the cop. "Oh my, let me taste this. Wonder if it's the right flavor and quality?"

The packets had been divided from a larger bag that had fallen behind on the floor. Strangely, another large bag of white powder had not been touched. This was not good for the pawnshop man.

"That's not mine!" He screamed in panic. Tears flowed down his face. He knew trouble was just about to begin.

"Whose is it, idiot? It really doesn't matter. It's in your establishment. I have you!" Smiled the police Sergeant. "Isn't this nice fellows? We now own a sweet little pawn shop and a nest egg of dope!"

"I swear that's not mine!" The small man sobbed.

Ignoring his words, the policeman continued, "Read the pip-squeak his rites and slip a nice pair of silver bracelets on him! He can get himself a lawyer and enjoy a nice stay downtown."

In a thousand searches, they had never anticipated the pawnshop could be a set up for drug activity. This could well be one of the major outlets for the areas drug industry that was getting nearly out of control. All law officers were searching for a means and way to save the city from this powerful activity. Children as young as six years old had already experienced the so- called thrill.

They were all happy to make this arrest. A cop stood the man to his feet, one placed cuffs on his wrist and read the words. The man kept quiet and didn't move.

The pawn shop owner was taken from the building and shuttled to a Police car. He looked pleadingly from the car window as it raced away.

Back inside the store, the customer was then questioned and immediately dismissed.

The salesperson was next to interviewed. As they spoke with him, he kept looking off. His eyes mirrored worry and his demeanor was fear.

"Alright, what are you hiding? You might as well come clean!" barked the Sergeant. "You know something! You might as well just tell us and save us tearing the place apart. It'll be best for you too!"

The man broke into a sweat and stared at the floor. He shifted his feet and sighed.

"One more time, make it easy on everybody. Give us a good cooks' tour and we'll let you leave. Your boss isn't here and won't be back for quite some time. We can tour or tear the place apart. Now would that not be a real shame?" Toyed Sergeant.

"Alright, alright! You'll let me go?" Squirmed the worker.

Knowing there probably was nothing to hold the man, the Police shook his head, "Yes, we will let you go. That is as long as you are not involved in his illegal business. You aren't involved are you?"

"Lord no! I try not to see stuff I shouldn't see." He admitted openly. "Sometimes I see things but I don't mess with it. He'd kill me!"

"You'd better be straight," Cautioned Sergeant. "Show us!"

"Up there!" He pointed. "That's where he keeps guns, money and different things of value. He calls it his vault! He just got that bag of stuff back there down. I see him go up the ladder for things."

Captain Williams insisted, "Lock the door!"

"Right! Let's get up there and take a look!" The cop decided.

The fellow was being very cooperative. He pulled a big ladder from the backside of the store beyond the showroom and sleeping area office. He positioned things in place and climbed quickly to the top. "Here! You have to push these ceiling tiles back!"

The onlookers groaned together, "Oh!"

He seemed to enjoy being a snitch and attempted to explain his actions. He rushed back down the ladder to talk, "What the heck, the old snake worked me like a slave. I really was a victim of his doings. He constantly threatened to kill me if I ever said anything. I even had to sleep in back. I was kinda like a guard but in a funny way."

"So you sleep here!" Captain noted. "Have to. At night he lets that big old wolfhound in back loose. He keeps him in that pen under the steps outside. He is one mean beast and I'm scared of him. Many nights I'd stay up on top of that shelf over there. The devil would get angry and chase me. He bit me a bunch of times until I learned."

"That scar on your neck from him?"

"Oh Yeah! I thought I was a goner that time! It took forty-two stitches. Mr. Ratton, my boss, told the hospital I was attacked by a neighborhood stray. They believed him and I had to have a bunch of rabies shots too. He thought they would take his dog. The taxpayers probably paid my bill. He's crazy, real crazy and he covers everything with being real quiet. He don't talk much and says talk is cheap and gets you in trouble."

"Can you handle this dog?"

"Oh no! I won't ever mess with him. He hates me!"

"Fine, we'll workit out." Smiled a cop.

The Sergeant made his way up the big metal ladder and stuck his head into the cavity of the ceiling area. A subfloor over the ceiling tiles was an amazing surprise. Along the walls were plywood shelves that gave inventory a safe refuge. Guns, money, jewelry and many valuables were carefully stored. In the middle area he had several small tables and a short stool. He swore to another cop, "Damn! Who would have ever known?"

"Well we know now!" The man rushed up the ladder to gain view. "This is something else!"

Sarge rebounded, "I'm calling the Chief, our Chief! Probably need the FBI too!" He mashed a button on a little box on his shoulder.

A female voice boomed, "Alright, Sir, any message?"

"Yes, send the Chief and Vice to the Pawn Shop. We need help. Tell them to hurry!"

"Ten-four!"

Captain Williams stuck his head through the ceiling opening out of curiosity. He cocked his head and whistled, "If you're through with us, we'll get out of your way. We need to get back to the station and write our report. Here's a notification to close this place. We have eight major violations. Our inspection should give you proper reason to be here."

"Perfect! We need that. Look at the drugs on those tables!" Sarge revealed. "I'll bet old Rattons golf partners are going to be shocked! It's going to be a hot time in our town tonight. This has to be a major bust! Can you get that watch dog out?"

"Nope! Call animal control, they can get the dogs, we'll stick to getting cats out of trees," Laughed Captain Williams. "We have to get back into service. Let us know how we can help. Have fun!"

"Sure! You have no idea how amazing this find really is! Thanks! This should be a giant step in saving our children!"

The next day, the area news was filled with the big "Bust" at the Pawn Shop. The Police were credited to full hero status. The firefighters praised them for their knowledge and efforts. It is a lot of pressure to be the ONE who tears at the drug Lords games. Firefighting is all about the CALL.

The day before had started out normal, it seemed. As it went on, they had to fuss with business owners to get their establishments safe and to code. It should be easy, and in some cases it was nothing. Always there has to be some who think they are "special" and above the law.

The Chief waltzed into the break room. "Todd, you've done it now!"

"What? I haven't even had time to do anything today!"

"Yesterday! You gave Miss Easter a ticket for her exotic panties being in the exit way. Oh yes, she doesn't want the fire hydrant in front of her front entrance. It needs to be moved. It is unsightly! She's going to the Mayor and City Council to get it gone." Shared Jerry Thomas.

"Good! Let the City give her the opportunity to move that hydrant. They are only about twelve feet deep. It would cost her several thousand dollars to get it done. Never say no to Miss Easter! As for those pretty panties, she keeps that table in the emergency exit and the door locked. That has to be dealt with. Every time we go there she has not changed things." Revealed Todd. "She wants the Chief to check her panties."

The Chiefs wife came puffing into the room with a huge box overflowing with great smelling food. She asked, "Whose panties need checking?"

The male firefighters looked at each other and turned red with embarrassment. Della tried to rescue the moment, "We did inspections and Miss Easter always has her panties for sale on a table in the Exit. Todd gave her a citation. It was Todd!"

"Oh!" She laughed, "What you people don't know is Jerry has a panty fetish! In college he lead all the 'Panty Raids' on our dorm. You younguns wouldn't know anything about that kind of thing!"

"Oh, yes I do," Confessed Todd. "I saw it in a movie! Looked like fun. Maybe we could raid Dellas' room sometime!"

"Just do it!" invited Della.

The pretty spouse smiled. She was constantly bringing her husband Chief goodies and when she did she always made plenty to share. "I have my special Chicken-Vegetable Stew for everybody. It's so cool outside. I brought you my Cheeseburger on the Run and that new cake, 'Blue Heaven'. I hope it will be good."

"Oh, thank you!" Della accepted. "Everything you do is always amazing!"

RECIPES FROM THE FIREHOUSE

E/Z CHICKEN-VEGETABLE STEW
(Serves one crew)

8 Chicken Breast (Filets or boneless) Clean well & cut into small hunks.
2 Quarts Hot Water
2 Teaspoons Sea Salt
1 Teaspoon Black Pepper
Place above in large pot. Cover with lid.
Boil on Med-High about 25 Minutes. (Add more water if need.)

While boiling chicken prepare next items:

6 Large Potatoes clean, cut into hunks.
1 Large Onion peel, chop coarse
1 Large can Whole Yellow Com/liquid
1 Large can Lima Beans/liquid
1 4oz. Can Mushrooms (Stems & Pieces)
2 Carrots chop in small slices
1-32 oz. (2lbs.) Swanson (organic)
Vegetable broth or Chicken broth.
PLACE ALL INTO CHICKEN POT AND BOIL.
Boil until potatoes are tender (about another½ hour). Turn heat to low.
MIX: 4 Tablespoons Com Starch into
½ Cup cold water.
Blend by stirring. If too thick add a little more water. Be sparing. This mixture needs to be thickish runny but not stiff.
POUR VERY SLOWLY AND STIR BRISKY TO BLEND. (Do not let it lump; slow mix smoothes. Don't break vegetables.)
COOK ON VERY LOW HEAT UNTIL THICKENED AND LIQUID TURNS A CLEAR-LIKE COLOR. (About 6 minutes).

If you want soup thicker you can mix a more Corn Starch and water as before and stir gently.

THIS KEEPS WELL AND IS A GREAT AND EASY/STEW THAT PEOPLE LOVE. Serve toasted garlic bread on the side. ENJOY!

CHEESEBURGER ON THE RUN

3 Pounds Ground Lean Beef (Salt to taste, use sea salt)
1 Teaspoon crushed Garlic
½ Teaspoon Black Pepper
1Tablespoon Olive Oil
1Teaspoon Dry or Deli Mustard
1 Medium Chopped Onion
1 Tbs. Texas Pete or similar sauce
1 Tbs. Worcestershire Sauce

2 cans Crescent Rolls or Hungry Jack Flaky Biscuits
16 oz. Shredded Med. Cheddar Cheese
1 cup Mozzarella Cheese
8 slices American cheese
6 Eggs Beaten
½ cup Milk
½ cup Sour Cream Pinch sea salt

PLACE MEAT INTO DEEP FRYING PAN AND ADD SALT. Stir and brown. (Don't let it get into big lumps. Keep it broken up to marble size.)

When done pour into colander and drain off fat.

Wipe pan clean with paper towel and return meat into it.

ADD: FIRST GROUP OF INGREDIENTS (Garlic etc.) Stir together over low heat.

USE 10X20X2 BAKING PAN or near size. Grease with the butter.

Open cans of rolls and line pan with them, on sides too. (Press together to keep mix from seeping out onto pan.)

SPRINKLE MEAT MIXTURE OVER PREPARED BAKING DISH.

Layer Cheeses one at the time over meat.

Combine: Eggs, Milk, Sour Cream & pinch of salt. Pour evenly over top of the ready pan.

BAKE IN PREHEATED OVEN, 435 DEGREES FOR ABOUT 20 TO 25 MINUTES. Let stand 10 to 12 min. Cut into squares & serve. Freezes well.

Later, microwave large squares, place on a bun ant take along.

BLUE HEAVEN CAKE

(Note: Wear plastic gloves because of cake color)
1 Cup Butter (Leave butter out of refrigeration overnight)
¼ Cup Crisco shortening
1 Cup Granulated Sugar
2/3Cup Brown Sugar
¼ Cup Hot Coffee (or use 1 Teas. Instant Coffee)
4 Large Eggs
2 Oz. BLUE CAKE COLOR
4 Tbs. Sour Cream
1 Cup Buttermilk
2 ¾ Cups Plain Flour (White Lily, best)
1 Tbs. Vinegar
1 Teas. Soda

MIXING DIRECTIONS:

Cream together Butter, Crisco & both Sugars (8 min. on SLOW in Mixer.) Mix in Hot coffee (to give fine texture) Add eggs one at a time and Cake Color. Don't over beat.

Combine milk & sour cream and alternate mixing with flour.

Blend well, then make indention and pour in vinegar and sprinkle soda.

It will foam. Then stir well into cake.

Preheat oven to 350 degrees and have 6 cake pans ready (greased & floured)

Spread mixed batter evenly among the pans and bake about 20 min.

ICING FOR LAYERS

2 Tbs. Com Starch & 1 Cup Water. Mix slowly over Med. heat until transparent looking. Set aside and let cool completely.

2 Sticks softened Butter & 2 1/2 Cups Powdered sugar. MIX TOGETHER WELL. Add 1 Teas. Vanilla Flavoring and Cornstarch mixture (Beat well by hand until smooth, then use electric mixer if need to let almost peak.

ICE THE CAKE LAYERS EVENLY.

Top each layer; let icing drip down sides.

*MAKE DRIZZLE: 1 Cup White Chocolate bits and ¼ cup Water. Microwave about a minute. Stir well, drizzle top and sides. (Add blue color) Sprinkle with dry coconut if desired.

CHAPTER EIGHT

"I'll never tell you anything again!" scolded Della with a laugh. She slipped the mini-blind aside to glance out.

"Why not? There are no secrets amongst us! We're family!" Captain Williams joked searching for endorsement. "Isn't that right Chief?"

The rest of the crew was listening and grinning. Fire Chief had just entered the room and held his cup for Della to fill.

"I didn't really mean anything by it Dell. That's just fact," Apologized Captain.

"Dumb ox, you could have just kept your mouth shut!" Della snapped. "They don't have to know that pawn shop idiot tried to mess with me!"

"Don't fret woman," grinned Todd.

"You took care of him."

"My gosh! I thought I had killed him," She trembled. "If I had, what would have happened to me? A murder charge?"

"Probably they would have said he attempted rape or something and let you go. But, had it been only a little grabbing and snatching then you might get life in prison or maybe the gas chamber!" Chuckled her friend.

Della stared at him coldly. "I ought to grab hold of you by the privates. And see how you feel about it!"

Todd playfully let out a yell and rushed toward her, "Oh, please do! Touch my body! I'll give you all day to stop!"

"Men! You jerk, you know what I mean," Della turned red. "He's a nasty ole ape that has no right to do something out of the way. It makes me cringe to think of it!"

Captain intervened quickly, "Della, he fell against something that could have killed him. Although an accident is an accident, it might have been a real problem." He cleared his throat. "Just keep your hands in sight when I'm around!"

Everyone laughed and winked at her.

They could hear the clear chiming of the town clock reminding them it was 1:00 p.m. Captain stood yawning,

"My wife made me a doctor appointment for tomorrow. I can't eat or drink after midnight."

"You never do snacks anyhow. You keep fit. Did you finish in the gym?" asked Todd.

"I did. By the way send a memo to everyone. The new treadmill is very fast. I nearly tripped. We need to be careful not to kill ourselves keeping fit. Are all reports complete?" reminded Captain.

"Yes sir," answered Della. "Did you read mine?"

"Its fine. Hopefully that's all in the past! I hope... "

The big horn interrupted. All the firefighters jumped for duty running to their stations at the trucks. They immediately crawled into turnout gear listening for the orders to come. With each firefighter in place, the two needed trucks rolled from the bay with all signals and whistles blasting. They turned north.

Todd was hanging onto the cross rail on the back of his rig. Ladders and other apparatus lined the sides over the many compartments of equipment. It was now beginning a heavy rain drizzle.

The older truck slowed and blasted the big horn just before the intersection and continued.

With the forward thrust, Todd felt his feet slide from the metal step area. He gripped frantically with both hands to hold on while trying to maintain a foothold. Bumping his shins, he screamed, "Help me! I'm losing it, I can't hold on!"

Wild eyed, Della came to rescue.

She jerked for his coat and snatched him upward. "Hold on!" she yelled, "Hold on!"

The vintage rig was coming to a slowdown that immediately gave a forward heave. Todd quickly caught the deck with one foot and pulled himself to safety with Della still attached to his jacket.

Her face was white, "Hold tight now idiot! We're crossing the tracks."

Without words, Todd obeyed by placing himself securely to the truck and engaged his climbing link around the safety bar. The old truck jumped wildly over the built up tracks with little speed. It swayed from side to side through the train crossing rushing to meet *The Call*. Once they were a block away from the train lines, a long black freight train roared its 200 plus cars through the corridor behind them. The warning whistles seemingly had been rather faint for its tremendous size. The ground still shook from the impact of travel.

"Look at that!" yelled Todd trying to be heard. "You saved my life, Della. Thank you! I could be laying back there under that monster!"

She gave him a thumbs-up and smiled. Soon the fire truck halted in front of a house that had smoke raging from an attic tower.

Everything was set aside to prepare for this encounter. Captain Williams placed both trucks into best positions each side of the hydrant and his men were fixed into place. His command center retained the usual readiness.

Without drama the firefighters would take their place in the effort to rescue this property.

The white spotted dog sat impatiently in his truck waiting anxiously for his time to work. He began barking when he saw the Chiefs white marked car stop near this rig. Chief Thomas and Captain Williams immediately began to determine their course of action.

"We're going in!" Captain stated.

"There are people inside trying to rescue their property. They have to get out. Somebody could get hurt. The smoke is getting real thick. Oh mercy! That odor, that's real weird!"

"You're right! Look, there's something else strange happening. That blaze there is an odd color!" Insisted Chief. "I'll order another fire unit. The power company is here now. Systems Natural Gas should be here. They never respond unless called."

Chief Thomas opened his radio to give orders to headquarters.

Captain Williams motioned to two firefighters and Mac to join him.

He pounded repeatedly on the door to no avail then stepped back. Bill Cross forced it open with a tool. Immediately they were met with a heavy smell of smoke. They checked their oxygen.

Power had not yet been interrupted. Lights were still on in the large house. This gave a limited view of the inside.

Williams called for occupants, "Hey, anybody in here? Yoah! Anybody hear us? Come on! We have to get everyone out!"

They were met with a nearby cry of an infant. Others were walking overhead. The people seemed to be unaware of any problem and were talking in muffled voices.

Williams located the infant and demanded, "Get this baby out of here!"

Firefighter Charles rushed to his call. Grabbing the little bundle, he started for the entrance.

"Hold it Mister! That's my young un!" called out a young girl.

He stopped in his tracks and Cautioned, "Oh? Come on, you have to get out too, now!"

She couldn't have been more than fourteen years old he guessed. Oddly, she was sitting on the floor in the nude. Charles knew this was an explosive situation in itself. There would not be enough caution to handle this minor female.

"Give me my baby!"

"You have to get out of here! Here, take this coat and cover up!" he ordered. "No, we can't!" she cried. "We ain't going! Put my kid down!"

"Captain! Come here!" panicked Charles needing advice. "She refuses to get out! She's 'necked'! What do we do?"

Williams smiled and stepped in, "For heaven's sake, get the girl out. We don't have time for games! Go! Go! Go! Take her any way you can. Give me the baby! Go lady or you're under arrest!"

The girl was hesitant but gave in to the order. She knew it was time to go and forced the coat around herself. As they retreated from the building an outside crew received the girl and her baby to let to firefighters return to the job inside.

"What on earth was that about?" asked Captain. "People are fools!"

"She has to be nuts sitting around nude!" Firefighter Charles added. He adjusted his oxygen mask as the smoke became somewhat heavier. They continued to appraise the first floor and found a wide twisting stairway.

On their way up they could hear voice becoming louder and clearer. Near the top, Williams could peer through the railings.

He stopped, holding his hand up and observed three men around a card type table.

One yelled, "You already took a thousand!"

"I did not! Count it again!" Roared the one with his back to Williams.

"Come on! We gotta make the split! There's not time to fool around. We need to get moving. That smoke is getting terrible!"

A white haired man with them tried to force a tactful plan. He coughed vigorously and wiped his eyes. "Timbo, I told you to wait to start the fire!"

"We're ready now if you'll give me my money!" argued Timbo. "A fair split is what we decided. Do it now! Give me my share!"

"I'll knock your head off if you touch that pile! You'll get yours asshole!" snarled the other fellow.

The white haired man intervened making peace, "Fellows, this is no way to act. Look here, we're all going to be rich! There's plenty for all! My favorite color, green! The silverware is downstairs and they have another safe there too."

The three began to rub their eyes and complain. They coughed and spit to rid their lungs of the powerful near invisible invasive murk. It seemed the room was deeper involved with the results of their created fire.

The old white fox reached for a fifth of liquor on the bar. He turned it up wincing as it connected to his tongue then handed it to Timbo. "Have a shot! It sure stinks in here. Hell, I can't take any more of this smoke!"

Timbo snatched the large bottle grinning, "My little angel-pie sure did fix us up. Wasn't she on the mark? Her dads stash was right where she said and he won't be back home for a week!"

"Hey, look on that dresser back there! That's a jewel box. I'll take that!" snapped the other fellow.

"Go ahead Skipper! You ought to be careful not to get traceable stuff. It could bite you in the ass!" warned white hair. "I'm going downstairs. I can't see with my eyes running! Dammit, Timbo, go put that fire out! You idiot! How the hell can we rob this place like this? I told you to wait!"

Williams held his group in place to observe. They watched the men stuff their pockets with the money. Time was closing in on them with the fire they had set. They had been so engrossed with their theft that their own safety had been completely overlooked.

"Wait!" whispered Williams.

"We'll get them!"

The fire crew wasn't sympathetic. The rush for making things right was roaring into their brains. They were almost crazy with desire to grab the three men and sling then out a window. In fire training had required they all would follow their leader and do the right thing.

Hoping to avoid confrontation, Williams motioned his men to follow and rushed onto the second floor.

White-hair spun around and caught him eye to eye.

Williams proclaimed, "This place is on fire! Come out now!"

White hair walked toward them as nothing was going on.

"Ain't no problem, we're out of here!" acknowledged Timbo grinning. "Get outta the way!"

Charles was near Williams as back up and others were mid-way on the staircase. The men coming toward them were cooperating whether or not they knew the depth of their plight.

Suddenly, there was a tremendous explosion that shook the house and area all around. Flames spewed high and jumped over the topside of the already burning house. Parts of the roof flew ruthlessly about and came crashing down.

The fire crew had placed the snorkel to battle overhead. Sometimes fires return to life even when they seem nearly contained.

From appearances, the fragile furnishings, years of memories and the past family life would now forever be altered. This rich home was coming to a sad end. Fire lines were everywhere and all the firefighters on this call were totally invested and working to control the event.

Inside, the stairway was ablaze along with other areas of the top floor. Now it was burning wildly with the robbers and firefighters caught in its midst. A second blast of whatever brought down more structure overhead and debris was scattered everywhere. People were shaken lifelessly to the floor unable to move, rescue or run.

Outside, Chief Thomas barked orders to his men, then connected to headquarters, "Send backup now! This thing has gone over the top! We need police, rescue, utility crew, and the works! It's bad. There were explosions too. There might have been a drug-lab here! Send it all!"

Chief Thomas rethought the episode and tried to place each occurrence in order of happening. The smoke, the fire, then the two huge blasts that are not common for a home environment.

He said aloud, "A firefighter never knows what is behind closed doors!" The Chief cleared his throat. "Oh God! Help us! This is real bad, real bad! My boys are inside!"

He didn't see Della when she raced to him. She Was desperately trying to be professionally calm but placed her hand on his shoulder. She puffed the words and stuttered, "Ch-ch-chiefl Captain Williams; Charles and some of our men are in there!"

"God, I know! Yeah! I know!"

"I'm going in!" she replied as a demand.

"Hold on!" Chief ordered. "Della, stop!

She refused to hear his command and kept going as if out of hearing range.

Todd joined her quickly, "Let's go! I got your back!"

Together they forced into the now smoke-blackened house. The only light was from burning spots and their flash lights. Their mutual goal was to rescue their partners Captain Williams and Fire fighter Charles and others who gave backup. They were only aware of them being prisoner to the lashing flames and deadly smoke.

Immediately Della heard a low moan and jumped toward its direction. In the process, her foot caught on a large boot that tripped her to the floor.

"Todd!" She called, "Todd, here, help me!"

He was by her side, "Take my hand!"

With one hand on his gloved palm, she could feel a body part with her other hand. Her heart raced with hope. "Todd, shine your light!"

Getting to her knees, she groped the figure to try to find a head by sliding her hand from the boots. She knew the fabric she was touching was tum-out gear.

"Captain! Hey, are you alright? Captain?"

Todd moved his light to the helmet and agreed, "Yeah, it is Williams! I'm taking him out! Give him to me!"

The firefighter placed a secure grip on his Captain and rushed him toward the half hanging front door. As he started out Della called, "Todd! There's somebody else here!" She again found the familiar turn-out material. "It's got to be Charles!"

Todd focused, "Dell, come on! We need help!"

"Go on! It's Charles!" She cried. "It's Charles! We're coming!"

Charles groaned and rolled over. "Please help me!"

Two more men in fire suits were nearby. One was fairly alert and the other was beginning to move.

She kept trying to get Charles to respond, "Can you get up or move! We have to get out of this place! Try hard! Todd will be back! You guys? Can you follow us? It isn't far to the door, maybe ten feet. Please, I can't do but one of you at a time. Help is coming! Charles! Help me get you out!"

The man gasp and started moving again, he grunted, "Oh yeah, just show me the way out! Oh! My leg is turned!"

Todd had rushed back to the door with his light. "Della! Come on!"

"I have Charles and two others! We're on our way!" Charles was half crawling and leaning on her. She stopped to check his oxygen.

The two other firefighters were struggling toward the light. Their gear was intact and they were overcoming the shock and surprise of things. They seemed to better off than they themselves expected.

Todd screamed with fear, "Come on! Now! Chiefs order! Now!"

"Almost there!" Acknowledged Della.

"It's dangerous in there! Thank God!" whispered Charles as he slid through the door. It had seemed like miles trying to get out of the dark dungeon-like mass.

Once the firefighters passed through the front door and were assisted to safety, there was another huge blast from overhead. Once more the house lit up with shooting rocket like flames as if the Fourth of July. The rumble of the house falling within itself shattered the hearts of the beholders. Firefighters, neighbors, and other crews were stunned.

Chief Thomas gazed in disbelief. He looked at his people who had just barely escaped the tragedy as they began to reach for the lifeline of drinking water. "Oh, thank you God!" Tears eased down his cheeks.

With all the extra trucks, personnel, and equipment on the scene, it would now be vital to maintain the building to burn within itself. Anything still could happen and they couldn't chance another blast.

Keeping the surrounding homes safe was urgent. Chief ordered the firefighters to keep the water flowing. They kept the pace endlessly.

The folks from the neighborhood who had assembled to see the event unfold watched with amazement and grief. The long standing home had been a token of history. With the feel of heat to their faces, they voluntarily moved back from the source.

As the fire lapped its hungry meal, one could hear the snapping, clicking, spewing, breakage and thuds from the building crashing away. It was obvious this would be a night of total work for every available firefighter.

Again, more trucks and assistance arrived from County volunteer units. They came to try to help redeem the now unredeemable. They sought out Chief Thomas who was nearly exhausted. Immediately, he gratefully welcomed their support and placed their efforts accordingly.

As with most fires, hours drag on and slowly onlookers give up and leave the sight knowing this would be a mark in history.

The news media from all around kept photographing and recording the story for the next News Break at their network. They knew not to interfere with the job at hand. Chief Thomas had years back informed them to observe and ask questions later.

"I'm fine!" contended Captain wiping a smudge of black across his face. He drank the comforting water offered him. Chief noted a paramedic insisting he place their oxygen mask on him.

"Take him on to the hospital! Look at that blood!" Chief quickly pointed to a wet blotch at his knee. "Get him out of here! We need our men in good condition."

They whipped Williams onto a gurney and strapped him in place for the ride. Once inside the medical unit, the big van rolled to the street with all lights and sirens sounding. They raced away.

Chief Thomas faced another situation that worried him. He faced Todd, Della and Charles who were wrapped in blankets in a near huddle. This was not normal. They looked bad, really unglued. They too needed special attention.

He motioned to another ambulance crew and said, "Take those three out too. They need hospital attention. Be certain they don't try to leave there. I'll send a car over later."

Della was nearly delirious and fought; then fell back listlessly. The other two were still coughing and blowing. The water that had been sifted over them brought comfort but was not reviving. The heat had been stifling.

Once more, another medic-unit raced off into the night with the three firefighters. The three were being carefully watched as they struggled to redeem themselves.

Todd whispered between the hacking and sniffs, "We've got to get back there, they need us! We were inside. We know what was going on. People were left in the house."

"There were other firemen on duty. They can handle it. Just relax! Give me your left arm! I need your blood pressure!" Demanded a beautiful lady in uniform. She reached for his arm.

Todd noted a cutting devise in her hand and pulled away. "Don't you cut my turn-out gear! This coat cost a fortune! I can't be without it! You're not touching it! Go on and do Della! She's much worse off than me!"

Understanding that Todd was coming out of his trauma, the medic turned her attention to Della. She checked her eyes, pulse and used the stethoscope. The medic was very serious and gave an order to Todd. "Get this coat off of her! Hurry!"

He obeyed and snatched it away from her body. Della seemed lifeless.

The EMT spoke in a shoulder mike. She whispered, "Move it, the female is in trouble. I need to start an LV. stat!"

"Got you! We'll be at General in about three minutes. I have a crew waiting there now. Dr. Peters is in the emergency waiting! Did you check the other two?"

"They're alright, a little tune up for them. Hurry!" She urged.

They tightened the belt around Della lying on the mobile board. Quickly she checked the oxygen and breathed a big sigh. Della still was not moving.

The box truck van rolled into a well-lighted drive and stopped.

"Oh, God! Please!" Begged Todd. "Please God help Della! You know how she gets in over her head!"

Tears flowed from the eyes of the two firemen as they confronted the fear of what gasses, smoke and extreme conditions can do to any one of them. Now, both Charles and Todd again prayed aloud together the Fireman's prayer.

As the loud ambulance stopped and doors opened, attendants met them to take over for the hospital. The flashing lights lit up the whole area around the emergency desk. They pushed the patient inside where orders were barked from person to person.

"Take her to room 101. I'll be right in. Get her vitals!" The emergency doctor demanded. "Who knows details?"

An ambulance medic quickly filled him in and turned over their paper trail. The doctor turned to the attending nurse and studied. "Call Fire Chief Thomas and check if this fire had any unusual chemicals or what might have put this patient in this condition."

Todd looked around to find the treatment room where Della would be. He noted the doctor and nurse studying a file folder of papers. Immediately he caught up with them.

He looked like the wrath of God from his own trip into the flaming mansion. Nobody could imagine he had been in such a fire situation.

The physician asked, "Can you fill me in on the statistics involving the fire?"

"Sure, Doctor. Several of us were inside the place doing our usual work. Della is the kind of firefighter who goes at it all the way. She found

Charles and another fireman and started to pull Charles out by herself. He's big and extra heavy with all his gear added. To top it all, she gave him her oxygen coming out. It's all very amazing but very dangerous too. She had to do it alone!"

"I need to know what chemicals were in the fire. Do you know that?"

"It was all burning, drapes., furniture, walls, floor and ceiling. The house was completely involved. They were to have killed the power and natural gas connections but I don't know the exact moment. The house blew up. We are all lucky to be here. Chief thinks the old back draft caught it. The thing blew a bunch of times. I don't think everybody got out!"

"No wonder you're exhausted. You people take too much risk then I have to put you back together. Why do you do that? Don't you understand life is about living not getting killed or nearly killed?" The doctor shook his head and mumbled, "Firemen! You refuse to take precautions for yourself!"

Todd was concerned for Della, "She will be alright won't she?"

"We're on top of things. Get yourself looked after. Orderly, come here! Get him out of here and in an examining station." Demanded the physician.

Arms suddenly hooked around Todd and dropped him into a wheelchair. He was whisk off to another place that smelled of alcohol.

It took nearly a week to get the fire totally finished. Three bodies were found in the charred remains.

Surrounding homes escaped damage other than minor smoke. Fire equipment was cleaned, sorted and returned to stand-by and all needed items to operate properly in its rightful place. The firehouse had every hose used laid out or hanging to render proper cleaning before returning to service or stand-by use.

The long conference table in the kitchen was occupied with the current working crew. They were to start their shift with Chief Thomas who was soon to arrive. The heads-up regarding this last amazing fire battle would be first on the agenda if the fire bells would allow and they could learn all the details.

The County Fire Marshal Brad Nelson soon walked in, pulled out a chair and slipped his paperwork on the table and nodded. He smiled accepting the cup of coffee offered. Every fire and tragedy was a part of his job He had to report and send reports to the state.

When Chief Thomas entered they were reaching for more empty cups to fill with coffee. He noted his men had a look of sadness and seemingly depressed mood. He could read each and every one of them. They had been together for many years and lived their work. He knew too that such a tremendous encounter as this last one would always take its toll on all, especially if someone had been killed, injured or danger was high. He opened his thick brief case as coffee was placed in front of him.

"Good morning!" he smiled gently. "We'll have a special briefing and discuss our findings on the Colonial Avenue fire. Let me first commend everyone on your superior efforts. You always make me proud!"

Everyone applauded him and it seemed spirits were lifted somewhat.

The sound of a vehicle stopping near the bay doors interrupted the meeting. They glanced around with anticipation. The kitchen door was recklessly opened and the crew stared in awe.

Before them roared in their missing firefighters, Captain Williams, Della, Todd, and Charles. They smiled big with open arms.

"You can't keep a good firefighter down!" Laughed Williams with gratitude. "That was really a rough one but we're here!"

Others yelled remarks to boost the observance of their return.

"That's right! Can't keep a firefighter down!" Smiled one.

"You're the tough ones!"

"Not really, they're the crazy ones! Not everybody could handle it and come out standing!" Chief Thomas praised. "We can count on you!"

From their hearts they rejoiced with the crew. Their pain was still there from the burns, smoke and pure trauma. They had narrowly escaped from the falling building and its back draft. To be alive was a true act of God.

When all reports would be completed, a tremendous picture would unfold. Life lost in a fire was always tragic no matter who the victim. Unfortunately, the men robbing the house designed their own plight. All for no gain and a pathetic death. Just somehow this time the innocent and the good did survive.

RECIPES FROM THE FIREHOUSE

DEVIL HOT TOMATOES

8 Med. Tomatoes (Firm & ripe) Peeled and quartered
2 Small Yellow Squash (Sliced thin)
2 Medium or 1 large Onions (sliced)
1 Purple Onion (Sliced thin)
1 Green Pepper (Cut into Strips)
3 Jalapeno Peppers (Cut very thin and leave in seeds) optional.
1 cup Distilled or Spring water 3 Tbs. Organic sugar
1 Tbs. Raw Honey
¾ Cup Red Cider Vinegar
½ Tbs. Sea Salt
½ Teas. Cayenne Pepper
½ Teas. Black Pepper
½ Teas. Celery Seed
½Teas.Oregano flakes
2 Teas. Mustard Seed
1 Teas. Finely Chopped Parsley

In a large glass bowl combine the first six ingredients. Set aside.

Use a Sauce Pan: Combine all other ingredients. Stir slightly and bring to a boil. Boil for about 2 minutes.

Pour hot over the vegetable mixture. Turn slightly with slotted spoon.

Refrigerate overnight or at least 6 hours to let flavors blend. Serve with slotted spoon.

The liquid left over can be poured over other cold vegetables later. Save in refrigerator for second use. Its better the second time around, try shredded lettuce and tomato.

OYSTER COBBLER PIE

This is one of my most favorite dishes, a connection to Seattle with its love of seafood. A must try!

1 Twelve-ounce Container fresh medium oysters (Salt with sea salt)
1 ½ cups crackers (Wafer Club Crackers best) (Or use pie shell)
½ CUP CRACKERS(extra)

Set aside extra butter for pie pan (need to be room temp.)
3 Green onions (clean, slice thinly; using 5" of the tops)
3 Tbs. Butter
½ Cup Evaporated Milk
3 Tbs. Plain Flour
1 Cup 2% Milk
1 Tsp. Lemon Juice
¼ Tsp. Fresh fine chopped Parsley
1Tbs. Ketchup
½Teas.Worcestershire Sauce
½ Teas. Black Pepper
Dash Paprika

Use: "High side" Pie plate or pan (with spill flange is good) 9" X 2"

1. Grease very liberally sides and bottom of pan with extra butter.
2. Crush crackers well, use 1 cup in bottom of buttered pan.
3. Drain Oysters (Set aside liquid) Place oysters evenly over crackers. Salt lightly. Chop onion and scatter over oysters. (You can add sliced mushrooms if desired.
4. In Medium pot, melt 3Tbs. Butter (Use med. Heat, stir in flour and blend together. Let cook a few minutes while constantly stirring. Add

both milks and stir to blend well over med-low heat about 3 min. Add oyster liquid and all other ingredients except crackers and paprika.

5. Pour over oysters in pan evenly.

6. Sprinkle remaining crackers over pie and top the crackers with paprika for looks.

7. Bake in preheated oven at 400 degrees for about 25 to 35 minutes.

8. Let rest for about ten minutes before serving. Garnish with sour cream and midget pickles. Serve in slices.

SHRIMP FROM HELL (HOT!)

(Stir-cook on burner or portable grill, good camp food)

1lb. Med. to large cleaned Shrimp. (Do remove the veins too!)
2 Tbs. Olive Oil
1 Tbs. Butter
1 Tsp. lemon juice
1 Small Onion, chopped fine
½ Tsp. minced Garlic Sea salt to taste
2 Tbs. Texas Pete
2 Tbs. Picante Sauce or Salsa
1 Tbs. Ketchup
1/3 Cup Water

Prepare all ingredients for use.
In fry-pan melt butter, stir in onion; let partly cook on med. heat.
ADD: Olive Oil, shrimp, garlic and salt. Stir fry to half done.
ADD: Lemon, Texas Pete, Picante, and Ketchup. Stir gently to mix and shrimp are fully cooked. (Pink outside)
ADD THE WATER TO MAKE A SAUCE.
Serve over steamed rice that you should have ready.
*Serves two people, multiply for additional servings.

INSTANT RICE

You can use a rice cooker and its directions. OR:
1 Cup white or brown RICE
2 Cups warm water.
1 Tbs. Butter
½ Tbs. Olive Oil
Salt to taste if desired.
Combine into thick Bottom saucepot. Bring to a boil. Stir occasionally with fork not to let stick.
Lower heat to simmer and cover tightly. Cook 14 minutes. Don't remove lid while cooking. At end of cook time remove lid and stir.
A good basic rice can be added to any meal. For more rice just make several amounts at a time.

SOUTHERN CORNBREAD MUFFINS

4 Cups Self-rising Com Meal (White Lily is my favorite)
1 Cup Self-rising White Flour (again, White Lily)
¼ Cup Sugar (Or substitute with a sugar substitute)
½ Tbs. Salt
1 Teas. Baking Powder
½ Teas. Baking Soda
3 Large Eggs (room temp.)
¾ Cup Crisco Shortening
1 ½ to 2 Cups Buttermilk (Use more of needed)
Have ready 2 large muffin pans well-greased with extra Crisco or if preferred, you can use well greased iron frying pans or loaf pans.

PLACE ALL DRY INGREDIENTS
INTO LARGE MIXING BOWL.

ADD IN: Eggs, Crisco and Buttermilk. With a gloved hand; mix and squeeze mixture until well blended. Don't over mix. It should not be real thick. If it is, add a little more milk. Use large spoon to put mixture into muffin pans or pour into other pans. Fill each muffin cavity ¼ full as they will rise.

*BAKE IN 420 Degree OVEN FOR ABOUT 25 TO 30 MINUTES.

Your oven may vary in degrees.

NOTE: * Southern Style often calls for "Cracklins". You may find them in some Southern Meat Departments. JUST ASK! They are pork bits Pre cooked and ready to use; sort of rare these days. Add to batter.

Most MEN love them, especially firefighters!

*Another Southern Style is add a can of Com. Stir into batter.

If you jazz up the batter, you will need to use well-greased pans not muffin tins but you can use half the batter to try things.

Some people like onions, peppers, olives, squash and whatever. Try it! SERVE WITH ANYTHING THAT GOES WITH CORN PRODUCT! Southern style is served with a glass of milk or buttermilk. Crumble the cornbread into it. Eat with big spoon! Love it!

Corn bread is great with beans and just meals.

CHAPTER NINE

Spring eases in opening buttercups and tulips first, then setting the buds on trees to cover the ugly from the past years fall and winter.

"It's a wonderful day!" Della chatted. "Daddy wants to plant our garden today. He wants me to help."

"How do you figure that? You're on shift!" remarked Gina Ballard.

"Correction, I'm going off shift at eight! You, friend are coming on!" Laughed the woman. "Once I finish this stack of paperwork I'm gone!"

"Maybe!" Gina snickered projecting she was in the know of some unique secret.

"Well, I love you too!" pouted Della waiting to be informed.

Leaning forward Gina whispered, "You don't know?"

"Know? Know what?"

"They're planning to change our shifts around. I think they want to mix it up all kinds of ways. Get you and Todd apart is most vital. Old Bailey thinks your group of NAZIS are after him!" Gina looked at a broken fingernail and stared.

"Want to know something? Bailey is half right, except for the fact we aren't after him. He's just not that important. He can screw himself up."

Della felt a tear roll down her face as she remembered overhearing Bailey pitching a hissy fit and ranting orally to himself. "I did hear him say it was too bad we lived after that last fire."

"My Lord! That's nuts!" Gina confirmed. "Well, he just-talks out of his head and wants to be noticed!"

"No, girl, he means it. That man is so into the bottle that he doesn't connect with the real world. He does think the world is against him."

Della provided. "He wouldn't kill but it would sure please him if we all kicked the bucket."

"We might all turn pale but we won't kick the bucket!" Gina consoled. She began to smooth out her uniform getting ready for roll call. "If he's on your case, I'm sure he double hates me because I haven't been here long and I'm a woman."

"I talked to the Chief the other day about the great Commander Bailey. He listened but said nothing except, 'He'll retire before long'. So you see we really have no place to carry our problem."

"What about the Mayor or City Council?" Gina asked.

"Oh no! That would reflect on the Chief. You know he's the best boss in the world! We'll just have to hang on." Suddenly Della broke out laughing. "Maybe our crew doesn't give the Commander his just due. They play every trick in the world on him and it makes him so angry that he goes ballistic. That's our power to hang to!"

"Well good for them!" Gina giggled, then looked serious, "It won't solve anything to change our crews around like the Commander plans. I'd guess it would make it much more difficult on everybody. We're used to each other. Looks like it would be like switching wives and families. It would be super to get on a shift with you but that won't happen."

"We'll hear the news soon. The Chief will have the last word anyhow!"

"That's right!"

"Dig this! I have a good one! I know some female firefighters who work in some other towns nearby. Let's get five or six of them to apply for some of the available positions here!" Della shared her new secret with a teasing sparkle in her eyes. "Ole Bailey detests women in the department anyhow. He told me many times I was just a 'token'. That flat burned me up, 'a token'! We work just the same as any other firefighter!"

"Of course we do!" Gina continued, "Last week Commander Bailey brought me his personal laundry from home and told me to do it for him. I was ready to tell him to shove it! Instead, we had a CALL. We were too busy for him to bring it up again."

"His Laundry? I'd throw it at him! That shallow jerk! He does need to get a life! Laundry! I suppose he'd want his shorts starched and ironed!

Actually that might be fun!" Della scoffed and shook her head. "Chief says he is 'old school'! Maybe we do need to educate him!"

They watched Todd walk in the door and rush to them.

Gina giggled, "Maybe he should ask Todd to clean his clothes."

"Whose clothes?" Todd puzzled reaching for the coffee pot.

"The great Commanders' clothes," Della flipped. "Poor soul has nothing to wear!"

"He can go necked as far as I'm concerned," smirked Todd slyly. "Come to think of it though, washing for the poor ole soul could be fun! Tell him I'll be glad to give him a hand. Dig it! What one could do for his comfort could be outside the bag! Maybe pink his shirts or sprinkle a little itch powder. Could even let him have the little lizard that hangs out at the back door. The little thing needs a new home and Bailey would have somebody to talk to!"

The women laughed as he mused about the possibilities that he would never try. Even so it all sounded like getting even had merit.

"Don't put him off on the lizard. Poor thing wouldn't ever know what color to tum. He'd have him sitting on all kind of bottles," laughed Della. "You know what he has planned Todd?"

"Changing our shifts!" blurted Gina.

Suddenly the sky blackened as it does in early spring. Rain poured lavishly onto the roof sounding like a freight train at full steam. As it cascaded down the high exterior walls, you could hear a steady drip from within.

"Dang! That roof is at it again!" grieved Della.

Immediately, Commander Bailey blundered loudly into the room and jerked a chair to the table. Della quietly poured him a cup of coffee and placed it in front of him.

Bailey made an indecent slurping noise then slung it against the wall. Everyone watched the cup crash into bits and fall to the floor. Grunting, he blinked with his blood shot eyes and belched, "God! Poison. and shoe leather, that's what you serve here! Look at that bread. It has most likely been here a month! Its hard as a brick!"

"Oh that, Sir, is not bread. That is biscotti." Gina proudly protested.

"Biscotti? Looks like it ought to be spelled with a *'P'* not a *'B'*," he chuckled. "Pisscotti!"

"Biscotti is a dry dipping sort of cake-cookie like thing. You develop a yearning for it. "You know, a gourmet item. Treat it like a sweet cracker," She advised rationally. "Try it. You can be sophisticated!"

"Alright, *so-piss-tocated* we will be!" Bailey smiled at his own pun and play on words. He picked up a piece of biscotti and snapped it into halves then sniffed it. "Well, I suppose the churches could use this for communion. It's hard as a cement block! Bet it will stick to the roof of your mouth for a month. False teeth don't do good with hard things."

"Dip it in coffee. That's what is good." Smiled Gina patiently trying hard to be nice yet not knowing when the shoe from hell would drop.

When Bailey chuckled with a moment of near friendship, the others let down their guard. Each reached for a piece of biscotti hoping for a social moment with their commander. They seemed to crunch at the same time.

"Mercy!" Grumbled Commander. "Sounds like a herd of horses!"

"Right!" Todd imparted with an even louder crunch. Suddenly it seemed to get very quiet, yet back to hearing the storms rampage.

"Did I hear a drip?" barked Bailey.

"I think so. It's that same place." Noted Todd.

"Todd get up into the attic space and see where it's coming from. You have to look during a rain to actually find the real problem. We've got one for sure!"

Todd sipped his coffee quietly dreading this new situation, "In a minute."

"No! I said now!" Freaked the boss. "Now! Now! Now!"

All the firefighters looked at Todd as he nearly jumped out of his skin. He said nothing but hastened to find the small rope to pull down the ceiling ladder that would get him into the attic loft. It seemed their good time was now over and hell would rise again. The hope had been Commander would have a nice quiet day and the firehouse would be spared some more of his antics. Once more, it would be full steam ahead.

Soon they uncomfortably raced to the sink and poured out their coffees. Everyone discarded their biscotti to the trash and dispersed the dishes into the dishwasher. The eight o'clock buzzer went off for shift change. They were ready for some to leave and the other shift to stay.

Commander Bailey leaned far back on the skinny legs of the kitchen chair and yawned, "Hey, sit down everybody! I need to talk to you, gals especially!"

Eyebrows lifted and the group of firefighters looked at each other with anger. The cleaning chores had been completed. Now they were to anticipate his next move.

"You know we're changing our shifts around. You're getting too personal and comfortable with each other. This place is not like home! This is a work place! You are to be ready to serve the city not each other. We get little 'clicks' and romances going. Some of you act like lovers and bosom buddies. Think it ain't noticed when you stick your noses together and sneak around?" Bailey began his paranoid tirade, "For instance, Todd is about to get on my bad side. I mean the 'real' bad side! Anything I ask him to do, sums up to be a damn burden for him. You've seen it, don't you agree?"

"Not really Sir," defended Della.

"Go ahead and defend that little devil! You're on thin ice yourself! I'll get the whole bunch of you fired and rid of!" He screamed nearly out of control with a face red as a turkey gobblers' head. "Gina, how about you?"

"You are sort of hard on him, Sir." She nearly whispered. "He just teases and tries to lighten some of our serious moments. He teases and plays with everybody."

"Well fine! Stick together! Women always stick together! That's what is wrong! Yelp! We need firemen not a bunch of pussy cats!" Bailey sternly quibbled. "I've always wondered what kind of female it is that always wants to do a man's job. Both of you ought to be finding yourself a man and get you a home and have babies. That's what you do! That's what God intended you for! He made you out of mans' rib and that makes you an extension of man. You just have to find the right rib."

Della cocked her head, "Oh! I need to find my *Adam!*"

Another firefighter scored, "That's one for the Commander. A dam and Evil!"

The women firefighters glanced at each other; color drained from their faces. They were biting their lips but knew to just let it go. This was a no win fight and to speak would only cause more irritation. They hung it up.

"You know I'm right!" stabbed Bailey. "Women ain't supposed to climb, ride trucks and *waller* with men on a job."

Della stiffened, "Commander Bailey, I'm sorry you feel that way. You cannot begin to believe how much being a firefighter means to me. It's my whole life and my world. I've worked hard to get here and I'm not going away!"

Bailey watched the tears swell in the eyes of both women and could see them flow down their cheeks.

"See! Women are weak! Look at both of you, squalling for nothing!" He grinned halfway. "I'm just kidding!"

"It hurts to be disrespected!" Sniffed Gina. "Actually, I'm tough when I need to be. I tear up when I'm angry. What's more, I'm a black belt too! How about you come and take me!"

Quickly she jumped in the middle of the kitchen and whipped through three Karate moves. She held her hands just so giving him an open invitation.

Realizing they were calling his bluff, Bailey worked to wiggle out of the pressure.

"Oh, bull! I said I was just kidding! You know we were just fooling around. I just wanted to see what you'd say!" He laughed and walked to the ladder going to the attic and yelled to Todd top side, "Hey boy! You find that leak yet?"

From what seemed like a far distance a muffled voice replied, "Maybe! Hope so!"

Commander Bailey was anxious to escape the possible outrage of the two females. He made giant steps to the iron ladder and began to climb still observing his path. "Good thing! Hey, what's this?"

"Can't see!" Mumbled Todd.

"Dang, it's a light switch! Well, how about that!"

Once he flipped it on, the area overhead lit up like a stage. Todd cautioned, "Be careful! Don't get between the rafters!"

"Think I was born yesterday? I built houses before you got out of diapers!" The older man snickered as he delivered his expert knowledge of the attic. "This is amazing! Look at all of these boxes. This is some place to keep things! I wonder who put it here! It's really dusty!"

"It might be just junk or maybe real good antiques." Acknowledged Todd from near the outside wall. He presumed it had all been there for years and it was none of his business. The station house was at least sixty years old.

"Sir, look here! The water is running down this wall from over there. Sure is a lot of it. Here is where it puddles over the kitchen and creates that drip. It has been running all over and standing. Down there is where it has made that water mark in the ceiling that you make me paint every so often."

"Well, no hell, Sherlock! Any fool can see that if he looks!" Growled Bailey.

"I'll bet its really coming off the side of the chimney. I can remedy it with some caulk and adjusting. It'll be fine!"

The Commander was more concerned with the contents of the stored boxes. He grabbed one and began opening the top. He grasps above himself to steady his failing footing on the rafters. An electrical wire running openly above him was a last resort. The wire snapped from the connecter and slipped through his fingers to its end.

"Holy cow!" the man yelled as an electrical shock dashed solidly through him, "Todd! The power! Cut the power off!"

Immediately his two hundred and thirty-pound body tripped into the soft water soaked ceiling. His weight and the sponge like tiles didn't mix. There was only one way, down! The tiles were cascading downward with Commander in the mess. At the end of the fall, he lay on the floor screaming for help.

"Oh, God! I'm killed! I can't move!" He blubbered and tears began to slide from his hazel eyes. The leather like wrinkles and heavy lines on his face protruded as he winced with pain.

Everyone had witnessed his plight. Assuming he was pulling another of his *tricks*, the two women firefighters began laughing and darted quickly from the room.

"Come back! Please! Oh I'm dying!" He pleaded. His face reddened and he wasn't moving. Suddenly, he seemed unconscious.

Todd carefully looked down the hole from the attic area then nearly jumped down the iron bars to the main floor. He squatted beside Bailey grabbed his radio and pushed a button that would connect him. A voice responded, "Go ahead!"

"Get an ambulance, Stat! Commander Bailey had an accident!" Todd requested with fear.

"It's on its way!"

The transmission created instant noise, then sirens and more help was coming. Meanwhile Todd was given his huge paramedic case while several others assisted as he worked to immediately treat the Commander.

Very soon an ambulance unit entered the truck bay with lights flashing. As routine the medical team raced to get their equipment and locate the emergency. Several firefighters directed them to the situation.

They followed while others opened doors.

Someone yelled, "Its Commander Bailey! He's over there!"

They could see him crumpled to the floor and Firefighters already at work on him.

Todd looked up, "He fell through the ceiling! We were looking for a roof leak. He grabbed an overhead wire and got a certain amount of electrical shock. I think the fall is the real problem. He has broken bones. Maybe his back or legs or arms; maybe he broke all of them! It doesn't look so good!"

Todd slipped aside so the incoming medics could take over. They loaded him onto a backboard and stabilized him for the trip to the city hospital. In minutes the vehicle was gone with the Commander inside.

The firefighters were nearly in a trance as they stared at the busted ceiling and the debris on the floor. Della and Gina were dumbfounded. They were quite shaken with the event.

"I should have helped him! God! I feel horrible! We laughed! I didn't mean to be like that!" Della grieved.

Todd soothed, "You didn't know what really happened! Nothing was your fault. He gets everybody so tom up, you don't know what to do!"

"I thought he was faking!" Explained Gina.

"Bailey grabbed hold of a live power wire to stop his fall. Nothing could prevent this. I hate it for him. He is hurt badly!" revealed Todd. "I'm going to the hospital. They might need one of us. I'm off duty. I should explain that wire to them!"

"Why's a wire such a problem?" asked Gina.

"When he grabbed the wire, he was probably wet. Sometimes that is very dangerous! Not just a simple shock but had he not fallen he might have had a worse situation." Chief Thomas injected. "You're right Todd, let's go on to the hospital. He needs some of us there. I'll call his sister so the family will know. We'll take my car. I'll be here today."

"What about our meeting?" Gina asked.

"That was some of Baileys' thing. We need to change shifts and get things in order." Stated the Chief. "Della, phone Captain Williams. He can hold the fort here. I hate to call him but he'd want to know anyhow. We will have to reroute some of our schedule."

"We're gone!" Todd nervously emphasized.

Bailey was still in the emergency room when Chief and Todd arrived. The doctor was writing on a large pad. He looked up and wiggled his lips, "He's quite lucky. His fall apparently removed him from the electrical surge he took. For all practical purposes he could have been killed. He is very lucky."

"Lucky? It really happened fast!" Muttered Todd. "When can he go home?"

"Not so fast! It won't be very soon. He fractured a leg and arm. We still are going to do more x-rays. We treated him for the shock and burn first. He was in so much pain we held off on getting too intense." Informed the physician as he watched a nurse carry out his orders with the patient. "We are waiting for a room now. Hopefully the medication will ease the pain and his fears. The man is very dramatically frustrated and hurting. He is lucky!"

"Lucky! whatever you say!" Todd sneezed into his elbow. "He really should not have come up to the attic space. I feel bad for him. This is so wild! Absolutely too much!"

The doctor nodded to the Chief to follow him from the room. He said, "I didn't know what to say in there. Chief Thomas, that man had been drinking alcohol prior this accident. I mean a lot. We checked his blood level. He probably staggered over himself. Being drunk makes treatment difficult. We have it in his records but we don't have to broadcast it!"

"I appreciate that Doctor, he's about ready to retire. We've all turned our heads in another direction to keep him from losing his retirement. He's been with the department over forty years, started when he was sixteen. He was just a kid. It ought to be worth something for all those years when he made a very minimal salary of about $35.00 a week. Back then you had to get up and go ON CALL from home at any time whether you were sleeping or eating." Chief sadly conveyed. "Now, he's still a good man but lost."

"I see! Here's what I'll do. We'll keep him here as long as possible. He has authentic injuries that can open avenues for therapy and council. I can do the papers to avoid the alcohol situation. He really will need every break he can get now. At his best, recovery will be long and slow." Sympathized the doctor.

"I'm sorry to impose on you. We appreciate your confidence and understanding. Lots of our men don't get along with him but I keep telling them he is soon to retire and to put up with him. He lost his wife to divorce recently too; just one thing then another. To get realistic, he doesn't want to accept getting old enough to retire either!"

"Most people have their greatest fear of getting old, or retirement. It can be near shattering to some. You know your life goes along a certain way and then you feel as if the rug is jerked from under you. One has to learn to cope with that factor in life. It should be to rejoice and look forward rather than considered an end. With him being a lifetime firefighter, it has placed him in such a massive masculine role that it will be most difficult to get him to understand that there is another real wonderful world out there, some people cannot cope. They may even create their own death. He will get help in spite of himself." The doctor explained.

"I appreciate your understanding!"

"To tell you the facts, the City would look bad with having an alcoholic on active duty at the Fire Department. People don't want to hear this about their heroes. That makes it more complex for him." The Doctor prevailed, "Consequently he chooses to live in denial. That is common too. But it makes for trauma and drama until some tragedy sets them back and forces them to straighten up for a while. Keeping his *secret* will work in our favor. I' II force him to desire the help he needs."

"Maybe we can get him into AA." Chief said.

"That is always good but he has to want to!"

"Keep me posted! We need to get back to the station. If he needs anything let us know. This certainly scared that kid with me to death! He is a sharp fellow." Chief extended his handshake and departed with Todd in step behind him.

On their travel back to headquarters Todd and Chief were quiet and deep into thought. Finally, Todd managed, "I guess he'll be back soon."

"No sooner than necessary! The Doc is onto his drinking situation," explained Chief Thomas. "He plans to force him to get help with that. Hopefully it will keep him in check until he does retire. Of course, he still has to deal with the broken parts from the fall. You know he will be wild. He'll be on crutches or a walker."

"I don't know anything that will control him. He did get a bunch of bangs and bruises this time. When he drinks he's nuts! He hates all of us especially Della and I. Can you think of any therapy that can help that? I knew sooner or later his luck would falter. He loves to live on the edge with fear and drama. He invites trouble. Like this, there was no need for him to get up into the attic. I was there!" Todd rendered.

The Chiefs car squalled to a halt. A big cat raced across the road with a fat Boston Bull on its heels.

"Hang on!"

"Slow it down! We can't have two more of us out of whack! Leave all the sickness to the commander!"

Chief grunted, "Sorry, I had my mind in left field. I keep going over the implications of this mess. It actually could get very complicated. Keep this in mind, if word got out Bailey was drinking on the job, I could lose mine. That's the rule. The city could consider me as being a party to it, in fact any of us who hide the fact.

"We'd better cover our tail feathers. At least none of us observed him taking a drink today, so that's something. Why don't you mention to the City Manager that he's been acting strange and indifferent for several months? Just say it for documentation. Maybe it will never come up anyhow."

"That may do the trick. That's what I'll do. One cannot cover a *drunk's* problem without trouble." Chief changed the subject. "How about that ceiling leak you were after?"

"It's not a big problem. I can fix it once it dries. Can get it done within the next few days."

When the two entered an open bay door, Gina and Della rushed to them.

"How's old Bailey?" They asked together.

"He'll be alright," Chief smiled with a twinkle in his eye. "He told me to thank you for that wonderful *mouth to mouth!* He said it was the best sugar he had ever had!"

"*Mouth to mouth?* Humph! That buzzard, he'd only wish!" Gina ranted raising her fist. "Yeah, I'd do *fist to mouth* to him."

"No you wouldn't!" Todd grinned. "It really looked like love! He is a new single man! Wait until everyone hears about this!"

"Do you want a hunk of this fist?" Gina returned the kidding. "Alright go on and tell what you want to tell, I really don't care! Shucks, maybe I will try to love the old fool!"

Things seemed to be returning to the old normal atmosphere in the station house. A little teasing could remove the severe edge of worry.

Gina continued defending herself, "Todd, you're a rat everybody knew I wasn't even in the room after ole *Humpty Dumpty* had his great fall. Isn't that right Dell?"

"Not sure, can't prove it by me!" Laughed the other woman.

"See! Who can you trust?" Snapped Gina.

Mac whined and barked, then rubbed his head against Gina's feet.

"That's right, at least I have you old boy. You are always the same friend from day to day, good, faithful, and trusting." She saw his black lips smile.

The loud buzzer broke into the moment and was followed with bells and instructions for the next CALL. From all directions in the firehouse, firefighters raced to their trucks for duty. They slipped into their waiting turnout gear and climbed aboard the waiting fire trucks ready to roll into action. No one was left behind except the dispatcher.

The bay doors automatically rolled up for the thousandth time and they clung to the radio to continue their instructions. Holding on as they turned the big left, they still struggled to stay in their places. Constant alert and care for the city was always the goal.

More horns!

More whistles!

More rush!

Being ON CALL was the focus and they were there.

RECIPES FROM THE FIREHOUSE

B. A. S. CAPTAINS' SPECIAL

(Bacon, Avocado, Shrimp) Serves 6

1 lb. Bacon, thin slice crisp fried

4 Avocados, perfectly ripe (To check ripeness: Feel the fruit gently. It should be slightly soft not mushy.

Remember not to bruise the avocado A hard avocado is tasteless and needs to ripen.)

4 pounds Shrimp (Clean, Peel and remove all veins) Boil in salted water until shrimp tum red. Remove to strainer when done. Let cool.

1 small chopped Onion

6 Hard Boiled Egg (Coarse Chop)

1 Teaspoon Minced Garlic

½ Cup Olive Oil

½ Cup Water

1 Packet of Salad Dressing Herb Mix (Four Seasons is best)

½ Cup Balsamic Vinegar

1 C4up Shredded English Cheddar

½ Cup Coarse Chopped Pecans toasted)

*Leaves of Spinach or Romaine Lettuce

1. Gently tum first three items into a large mixing bowl. Set aside.
2. Mix together next 7 (seven) items then pour over first mixture gently.
3. Layout leaves of spinach and or lettuce. Do this in even clumps for individual servings.
4. Sprinkle cheese and pecans over.
5. Garnish with Grape Tomatoes.
6. Serve with crackers, flat bread, or Texas toast. Enjoy!
You can switch Shrimp for Crab, Chicken or Tuna.

WONDERFUL SHRIMP BISQUE

Great to serve with this is a cup of bisque. Use 1 quart of Shrimp broth add:
2 Tbs. chicken powder soup
4 finely chopped green onion and stalks, 1 chopped celery stick, salt & pepper to taste. Boil 20 minutes. Add a cup skim milk, stir. Serve in cups.

FIRE CHIEFS' BANANA PUDDING

1 1/2 to 2 Boxes White Butter Cookies or Vanilla Wafers
6 Pounds, more or less, Bananas, (Use barely ripe) Slice thick.
Place in large glass serving bowl, alternating layers of Cookies and Bananas, (Cookies first layer, etc.) Set aside.
PUDDING MIX:
3 Medium Eggs
½ Cup Water
1 Can Evaporated Milk

1 ½ Cups Granulated Sugar
2 ½ Tbs. Corn Starch
1 teaspoon Pure Vanilla Flavoring
1 teaspoon Almond Flavoring
1 Stick of Butter, melted (Do not brown)
PLACE: Eggs, Milk, Water and Sugar in top of double boiler.
Beat with hand mixer to blend sugar.
ADD: Corn Starch and flavorings STIR IN: Butter
Bring water in bottom of double boiler to full boil.
Place Pudding Mix over the bottom half of the boiler. (To piece of unit)
Watch for Pudding to come to a boil, stir constantly or beat slowly.
When thickened, pour while still hot over Cookies and Bananas.
YOU HAVE MUST MADE THE BEST!
Serve in small bowls with Whipped Cream.

HOME MADE WHIPPED CREAM

Make your own! Use 1 pt. Heavy Whipping Cream and beat with heavy mixer. (Wire attachment) Cream must be very cold but not frozen.

When cream is almost a ready thickness, sprinkle in about ½ cup granulated sugar and beat to dissolve and finish.

(Take care not to over beat as it will turn into butter.)

SERVE OVER PUDDING OR WITH ANY DESSERT.

SUNDAY POTATOE SALAD

(Make ahead to serve cold) 5 pounds White Potatoes
(Peel and cut into small squares. Wash well after peeling)
Have large pot of boiling salted water ready.
Boil slowly until firmly soft. Taste one, you will know when it's done.

Pour off all water and let drain (colander). Salt now to taste. Don't handle potatoes any more than necessary. Makes them mushy. Set aside.

PLACE IN LARGE MIXING BOWL:

1 medium fine chopped onion

1Tbs. Minced Garlic

3 Tablespoons Mustard (spread type)

2/3 Cup fine chop sweet pickles, plus

3 Tbs. Pickle juice

1 Tbs. fine chopped fresh Red Pepper (optional, for color)

1 Tbs. fine chopped fresh Yellow Pepper (Optional)

10 Boiled Eggs (whole) Chopped medium.

1 Tablespoon White pepper

1 Teaspoon Celery Seed

Mix this together gently.

STIR TOGETHER POTATOES AND SECOND MIXTURE

2 Cups Mayonnaise (more or less) Hellmann's or Duke's are excellent. Add Mayonnaise by turning in gently, least handling always best. (Easiest is put on gloves and tum with hands).

PLACE IN GLASS CONTAINER WHEN IT SUITS YOUR TASTE AND LET IT HANG OUT IN THE REFRIGERATOR.

Potato salad is always best after setting aside for a while.

When ready to serve, place in a serving bowl. Quarter several fresh tomatoes and have ready lettuce leaves for embellishment.

CHAPTER TEN

"Sure, we'll look forward to seeing you then!" Della slammed the old phone into its perch. She was nearly out of breath. "Wheesh! That's everyone! Can you believe of the thirty women in this area that work in fire departments and only two of us have made firefighter? They are usually hired for office help and public relations jobs."

Gina gave a concerned look. "We could be crazy! We most likely should worry about our own positions and not rock the boat. If the other females want to be a firefighter, why not let them figure it out. That's what we had to do."

"Maybe so, but as a woman I believe strongly in equal opportunity for all!" Della lifted an eyebrow. "The head honch has dare not say too much to their *tokens*. It certainly wouldn't look good. If you really consider the facts, it is time that some of the firefighter jobs here be open to other women along with the eligible men. There are some very qualified people available and we need to help make it happen for women too."

The two smiled as they watched the male firefighters in the kitchen struggling with lunch preparation.

"Well ladies, can we tempt your group with *FIRE HOUSE CHILLI?*" invited Todd, "It's hot! Believe me! MANHOT."

"Man what?" Della snarled.

"Man hot?" Blasted Gina. "So what does *man hot* mean?"

"Just a dumb ole thing, I suppose," Todd dropped his head looking like a scorned puppy.

"Yeah, put out the bowls, idiot!" Challenged Della knowing the meeting of 'Women in Fire Fighting' would begin when the group arrived for their data on jobs available. "We'll all try it!"

"Great! We have a huge pot cooked! We could feed a platoon! It'll be ready within the hour." Bill Cross reported as he placed bowls and spoons around the table. "Get the napkins, Charles."

Bill Cross and Charles Boyd were two firefighters who had been transferred into Station One back in the winter. Due to the schedule and the heavy calls to this firehouse they had been sent to fill in for the needed new personnel. Quite often governmental groups postpone hiring until the demand is nearly out of control. Them being at Station One meant their previous stations were left shorthanded. It never seemed quite the same to be a fill-in.

Charles replied, "Good, here are the napkins. I'll make a few gallons of tea; we'll need it! Can't you imagine the newspaper headlines tomorrow: *BIG CHILI FIRE AT STATION ONE, SIX ALARM! Put out by ten gallons of tea!*"

Charles laughed loudly and was joined by several of his mates. As he started out the door he heard Della screech, "Hurry back and bring me some buttermilk. I'm making Grandmothers' LACE CORNBREAD!"

"You know how to get to a man's heart! My grandmother used to make that too!" Bill recalled.

"Run across the street and get four cabbage heads. This requires slaw! Bring mayonnaise too." Captain Williams flipped a bill on the counter and nodded to Charles. "We're always out of mayo!"

The rest of the firefighting crew rushed into place as they often do. Each wanted to add their part in making this lunch very special. As they began pulling the details together, the Women in Fire Fighting began to arrive.

Very soon, twenty-four females sporting different uniforms or civilian clothes arrived. Della organized them to find their seats in the big kitchen conference room. Two tables were set properly and little wild flower centerpieces gave a supporting welcome.

The complete Saturday lunch was ready to be served. Todd muttered to Charles, "Dum! Looks like we'd pray before feeding this crowd. Remember how they *fed the multitude in the BIBLE*, except we don't have fishes and loaves?"

"No sweat! This will work well. We'll split this into two pots, to one batch we'll add the heat from hell and make it so hot they can't handle it!" Planned Captain Williams. "Get those plastic soup bowls to serve the females. See how easy, ladies dine with the red ones. Watch the special potion! Women can't keep up with us. Quiet, here comes Della!"

The crew gathered around laughing as if they had *short-sheeted* a palace of beds. Firefighters love to play and this was special.

Crewman placed the bowls in front of each female. Captain smiled widely. "Ladies we insist to be great firefighters you have to be able to handle our *CHILI*. It's perfect! Here comes the tea! Everybody needs tea! Pass the cornbread and slaw too!"

Gina started the serving by placing her cornbread and slaw on a side plate. The lace cornbread was toasty brown and enticing. "My Momma makes this but not so beautiful."

The guest joined in.

Todd was amazed to see most of the one big pot of *hell hot chili* disappear. The men were served in the blue bowls from the second pot of the milder version.

The resident firefighters sat amongst the women and filled their plates to the top.

At last, the Chaplin prayed a short thanks for the food and blessed it to their continuing health.

It was now time to eat and the aroma was extremely inviting.

Unsuspecting Della spooned her first large bite of chili into her mouth. She felt the water form into her eyes, her nose burned and her lips went near numb. Grabbing the tea, she moaned loudly, "That's hot! MANHOT!"

Cornbread became the second bite. As others watched, they followed her lead.

The house crew was snickering at the situation. They winked knowingly at each other and the more they thought about it the funnier it seemed. Watching the females try to eat the stuff was a real hoot to them.

Della whispered to Gina, "Slow down, just eat bread. Pass the word."

Todd and Charles clapped their hands to the table, snorting in glee.

A phone rang in the kitchen. Della jumped to answer it quickly. "Thank God you called! I needed to get out of there. Come on and hurry! Gotta go here comes the Chief!"

"How's your meeting going?" Smiled the tall straight man.

"You won't believe this! Todd, Charles and Captain have spiked our chili!" She revealed.

"Spiked your chili, with what?" He asked with a grin. How is that possible?"

"They knew we were having the W.F.F. group meeting. They decided to have Chili for lunch. They invited everybody and dumb old me fell for it. This is without a doubt, *Chili from hell.* Its so dam spicy hot, I'm afraid it's going to eat the bottoms out of our bowls! Its Six Alarm for fact!" She relayed. "They are truly a bunch of jerks. They almost became sane!"

"Go back to the table, I'll take care of it for you." He assured.

Della eased back to her place and nibbled the Lace Cornbread. She noted the other women were doing the same.

Chief dipped a big bowl of chili as they watched and sat beside Captain Williams. He had a blue bowl with the good chili. He tapped his glass with a spoon and held it up. "Alright folks, I'd like to welcome all of our guest! It's an *old fashion fire department custom to toast* new friends and I see quite a few new faces here. Let me suggest we toast to trust! Let's lift our tea and together salute, TO TRUST!"

Baffled but cooperative, the room full of squad and guest saluted as ordered.

They yelled together with their tea held high, "TO TRUST!"

"Now to prove you have our trust, I want each of you crewmen to exchange bowls of chili with the guest closest to you. Yes, switch with the lady in the W.F.F nearest you." Urged the Chief Thomas. "Do it and show your total trust. We have needed to fill all of these job positions here and this is a great place to start. After all, TRUST is one of our most needed asset."

It seemed crazy but at times the Chief could get as crazy as the next. The exchange finally began to happen. The women smiled happily knowing the fabulous Chili would be theirs

Looking at each other in shock, Chief laughed and picked up his spoon, "Eat up!"

Todd had slid his bowl to Gina to exchange with her. "Oh, God! We should never have done that!"

The women on their mission had been saved. They were cleaning their plates and bragging on how wonderful everything was. Several wanted more.

Finally, Todd, Charles and Bill Cross jumped up trying to drink tea at the same time. Todd pleaded, "Come on! We forgot that inspection at the square!"

"That's right!" Agreed Cross.

"Oh sit down!" chuckled Thomas. "I canceled it!"

"Oh, hell! This is hell!" Todd grumbled. 'Please! We'll confess!"

"Confess?" Della lit up.

"Yes, confess!" he gloomed. "Confess!"

"I don't understand, what do you mean?" Gina probed.

His eyes were red and brow was dripping with beads of sweat fired up from the heat of the *Chili*. Todd kept stuffing cornbread into his mouth and slurping tea. Folks watched with interest.

Captain quietly perspired but ate casually being careful to dilute the *Chili*. He too rushed the browned lace bread and tea. Suddenly he felt miserable and wanted to burp. "Oh, my!"

At last Todd laid out his confession. "Mercy, I'm sorry! Real sorry! It was so nuts to try to put you on! We thought *Six alarm Chili* would be a fun trick. It started so innocent, like we would be the high and mighty if we were able to eat this hot stuff and you girls couldn't. Uh... well, uh... this is really embarrassing and stupid!"

Captain added, "Women are women and men are men. We thought it would make us look better, so we tried to tip the scale. Still, we all know women are great firefighters. We desperately need more people working here. This was just playing not meant to be degrading to you."

Todd blubbered, "You know we really want you. We do need..."

"Todd! Stop!" Chief laughed. "We get the picture! Just reach up and jerk your foot out of your mouth!"

"Dang it... I am sorry.' It, uh... uh... sort of happened …. uh! Well, anyhow I had help. Captain and the others joined in," He tattled.

The crowd laughed, watching those in the hot seat try to repair their backfired *joke*.

The Chief stood, "Ladies and guest, the men are trying to say they are embarrassed, feel stupid and brainless for this crazy trick. They love to play with each other so it is something to consider as a natural thing for firefighters. You do understand this?"

"Normal is short-sheeting your bed during your first shift!" injected Della grasping the moment. "Maybe if they do all the dishes, cleaning and buy us ice cream we'll forgive them!"

"Yes, we can forgive them, they are *human men!*" Another woman from W.F.F. spoke up. "At least almost forgive them."

"Della has the best idea. Earn forgiveness!" Reminded Gina.

"It was a wonderful meal for all of us. With a little fun injected, we were saved by the Chief!" Della giggled. "Get the ice cream!"

The sound of buzzers and alarms broke the moment. Duty-personnel were literally saved by the bell! While the crews were jumping into their turnout gear and finding their places on the trucks the announcements were being announced over the house speakers and monitors.

The building vibrated with the roar of engines as three trucks rushed through the open bay doors to discover the action. Once the firefighters and their trucks were on the street, the building became near silent to compare.

Della left with her team too. Only the W.F.F. members, the Chief and a few other staff remained at the table in the conference room.

Fire Chief Thomas tapped a musical glass for attention. "Well, you just received a quick lesson in what we really do here. I know this is not totally new to many of you, but remember this is constant. Most often our meals are interrupted by THE CALL and we have no idea where or what until we get to the scene.

"This fire house takes a lot of people, team players with deep courage to carry on the details of each run from the station. It is a high profile job. Every firefighter who comes aboard with us must be sincerely dedicated. You must be willing to learn new equipment, technique, new ideas and school constantly. Your love for each other and the people in this city will motivate. That's the nutshell of it. Here are some job applications. If you believe you qualify take one, fill it out and return it in three days."

Chief Jerry Thomas stood and smiled. He looked directly at each of the W.F.F. ladies and continued, "I've got to catch up to THE CALL. Please finish your meal. We may be right back, depends on what's out there. Sometimes it goes on for what seems forever."

He immediately left and rushed for his car to follow his people.

A tiny blonde about twenty-five reached out, "I want one of those applications. I can do this!"

All others quickly scrambled to receive one of the four-page job enlistment forms. Once they returned to their places they glanced at the many questions.

Gina was still at the station and took charge, "It'll take quite some time to fill this out. Do it slowly and be accurate. Let me give you one pointer, every potential employee of the city will be given a drug test and a background screening. You will also be expected to pass a medical test too."

"That's right nosey!" One woman remarked.

"This is a career you're reaching for. There are seven firefighter jobs and other city positions available. This is a real opportunity. Give it your best! Do remember if you use drugs or alcohol to excess it will show up. Let me say, if you have that kind of problem, go for help now and apply at a later date."

Three women laid their papers down on the table. They seemed sad. One stood and said, "I've got to get back to work."

When she left the other two followed behind.

"That took guts!" Gina sighed. "Maybe we can still help them get ready for the next time."

The group chatted while finishing the meal. A WFF lady asked, "Are we going to take a tour of the station?"

Being left in charge was satisfying for Gina. She felt important. Della had shared her knowledge making a tour easy and fun. When they entered the bedroom area the women looked at each other.

One woman turned white and nervous, "My ... my gosh! Do we sleep with them? There are three beds in a room!"

Gina grinned and explained, "Oh, no, in fact when on shift you have your own private bed and room. You are assigned this. There are three shifts, so the rooms are shared but per shift. See, there is a private bathroom per room. We do have a few barrack type rooms too for males and sometimes visitors from other departments. Years ago women didn't work shift, they could only work day hours."

"How wonderful!" Smiled a tiny blonde lady.

"The department has a great exercise room. We recommend our people to take advantage and keep fit. It's important to keep in good physical condition to help stay on top of the job." Gina informed.

"Amazing!" A redhead exclaimed. "I'd love this! I need to lose a few pounds!"

The reasonable quietness was interrupted with the groaning of trucks outside and the bay doors opening for the returning crews. Excitement mounted with the quick return of the firefighters.

Gina ushered the visitors back to the break room. The Chief entered immediately in a quiet mood. He said, "Ladies, I hope you enjoyed your lunch and visit. Feel free to return your application. We are hiring now. We need to have a department meeting in here now. Thanks for coming."

The women quickly said their goodbyes and quickly departed for their cars. The crew entered and found chairs.

Chief scratched his head watching the activity. He thought out loud, "Out of about twenty-five, we might get one!"

Todd slid into a nearby seat, "Chief, what do you think, some group of chicks? Huh?"

The man smiled at his young thoughts. "I've seen many more male hopefuls in my day, maybe not that many at one time. You've got to say they really have passion for the job. Lots of courage and spunk!"

Captain added, "That's the word, *passion*. I love passionate women! They are hard to come by."

Della overheard the review and snapped, "You're simple! Women are complicated, you just don't know. True, we are firm in our dreams and beliefs. I'm here! Look, see this badge? This says firefighter not *woman!* We had better be passionate or somebody could lose their all! Remember? It is dedication to the force and all its needs."

Todd tried to gain face. "We are so spoiled with you and Gina, there is nobody like either of you. You pull your weight and go the extra mile."

Della flipped her head and tried to smooth her hair from the helmets special pressing. She narrowed her eyes. "Maybe not yet! It takes time to become that great firefighter and team worker. We have to give everyone a chance whether a man or woman! We can't start at the top or we'd all be chiefs."

Again the Chief tapped a glass to bring all to attention. "Alright, we need to go over the details of this last car fire. We have some new procedures to discuss."

The meeting lasted nearly two hours with intense discussion of what future fire calls for vehicles would be. The city had changed some ordinances that applied to their work. They had to be up-dated with the paper work and spell it out so as not to take the chance that anyone would not understand this new information. The Chief would lecture all shifts throughout the department.

Just as they completed the final questions on the new procedures, the loud buzzer began its urgent call. Again all personnel rushed to their post to grab their turnout gear and settle into their place on their truck. They listened to the overhead speakers for some direction.

Bay doors automatically lifted and once more the sirens screamed their urgent warning that they were heading for The Call.

This time three trucks were dispatched to a home fire in the ghetto part of town. With an area of poor housing and blocked streets moving the trucks into place would be more difficult. Upon arrival they could see it would be a long night for the department. It would require special force to contain an already spreading hot fire.

Immediately they could see a woman pacing in front of the roaring blaze that seemed to leap wildly from broken windows. The lady was screaming frantically, "My baby! My baby! Where is my baby?"

Quickly, Della rushed to her to obtain any vital details, "Please calm down! We are here to help! Please, tell me, where is the baby?"

"I saw her last in my bedroom up there!" She pointed. "I tried to find her! I tried to get her! I lost her in the smoke!"

"Tell me, where is that room? I can get her! The room! Where?" Pleaded Della

"Up those steps in the back side, across the room beside the closet. Please, she can't get out, she's one-year-old! Help her!" She wept and shook helplessly.

A neighbor walked up, "Margaret, Hold my hand and pray! Come on!"

A firefighter with Mac pushed the two to a designated area for onlookers and continued to watch the people.

Della caught up with the Captain and explained, "There's a child inside. I'm going in that window over there. Cover me."

"Alright, we'll shoot you up with that ladder. Don't take chances!" He cautioned. "Go easy! We'll start someone inside from below! If it's too risky back out!"

Todd screamed, "Della, No! Don't go in! It's too far gone!"

He started up the ladder to back her up. She was already rushing inside the glowing smoke filled window. From her view, Della knew she only had minutes. Protected by her turnout gear and breathing devise, she knew the crying child could only be saved within the moment. Without hesitation, she followed the crying and coughing in the smoky dark room. Quickly she grasped the baby and rushed back to the window. The child was very small making the rescue easier. There had not been time for oxygen, only time to run.

Once on the ladder and way out, Della yelled, "Captain, Catch!"

He was ready and caught the frail bundle. Medics were at his side to follow with proper help. Immediately oxygen was given and the baby was placed in an EMT unit.

The firefighters continued to battle the blazing inferno as it ultimately began to shatter within itself. It wasn't long before the roof and the overhead structure fell into the area from where the child had been saved.

Black smoke spiraled in an upward roll as if smothering the blaze. They all know you can never trust the beast.

Hastily, it rekindled and the totally involved the building of heat from hell pushing the fire line back to the other side of the street. The crews kept drenching water on surrounding homes and buildings for protection from the boiling heat. The final fix on this house would take major effort to bring it to a final end. This was not unique to the job.

EMS had carefully attended the little child who had been rescued by Della. Oxygen had given her new life it seemed. The mother was on her knees crying. She sobbed, "Oh, thank you! Thank you for being here. You saved my baby! I don't know what I would do without her! Oh thank you!"

As time passed on, several others needed help from the EMT and special consolation from various ones who could console them about their loss and the tragedy that major fires create.

It was a long tedious battle but finally it was controlled. They won! New and fresh fire crews were sent to replace the tired and weary firefighters who had wrestled the intense fight.

News media slipped into the area and quickly set cameras to lavish a story for the public. Knowing Della was the hero of the event, they wanted to start the interview. Della was black streaked from sweat, smoke, soot, and water. She wanted to run but smiled, "This is not my usual make-up!"

Ignoring her desire for privacy the broadcaster laughed. "The heroine of this day is Firefighter Della Jones. We understand you rushed up a ladder and went into a window and pulled that little baby girl out of the burning home!"

Della took a deep breath and pushed her hair from her face, "We all worked together for this rescue. Captain Williams and Todd my partners were right with me! Not only that, the ladder crew put me to the right spot to be able to find the child. EMS was in place to help the baby recover the trauma. It takes a team to be a hero! We all work together for each rescue."

"But you went inside for her! That's amazing! Even more amazing, you're a woman firefighter!"

"I've been a firefighter for twelve years. We just take turns at all fire events whatever comes up we partner up to handle it." Della smiled receiving a warm white towel from one of the EMT persons. "The department has the best fire crews anywhere and I'm proud to be a partner. We all work together to cover all our cities' needs. We want our people to know we are here for them."

The reporter smiled, "What do I say? Congratulations to the whole crew and department and especially you!"

"I guess. Thank God! Luck was on our side today. It's a wonderful feeling to be part of saving a life. Things can be replaced but lives can't, they have to be saved!"

The reporter grinned cheerfully, "I know the child's mother is grateful and we're truly in awe. Thank you from the heart of the city. We need more women like you with the knowledge and stamina to handle this job!"

Della looked down then in the eye of the camera, "Our place in the city fire department is to know what to do and do it. Any of our firefighters would have done the same. We have a top department and stand ON CALL 24-7!"

Finally, the trucks were packed to return to the station. A unit was left overseeing the ruins for safety. With intense calls, it's vital to keep people safe and make certain the flames don't rekindle.

Della stared from her seat. She could see the child and mother wave goodbye. Her tired hand waved back. Tears of relief dropped onto the smoked turnout suit. She smiled at Todd who watched from a mirror.

RECIPES FROM THE FIREHOUSE

FIVE & HALF ALARM CHILI

(Serves about 28 to 30 hungry just returned to duty firefighters)
8 pounds' lean ground beef
2 pounds' sausage (cheap brand best)
2lbs. Ground turkey
1 1/2 sticks butter
Place all above ingredients into oil sprayed pot (large) or deep iron pan. Stir constantly while cooking on medium high heat until a little brown and yet some not totally done. (Best if you keep some random lumps no bigger than the size of a quarter. You don't want texture too fine.)
Pour off extra oil and grease or drain in colander to remove excess fat. Good to let drip-drain over bowl. (1 brow the drain off into your compost, never the sink drain!)
Find a huge pot, maybe a canner but very big. 20 quart is great! It will need a snug lid and headroom is important!
Pour drained meat into this pot.

NOW ADD:
3 large Onions (medium chopped)
3 Tbs. Black Pepper
1 Cup Yellow Mustard
2 Cans Beer (Your choice)
2 Large Green Bell Peppers chopped
2 Cans 4.5 oz. Green Chili Pepper
8 Tbs. Minced Garlic (in liquid)
½ cup Granulated Sugar
24 oz. bottle good Ketchup
2 large Tomato Sauce
2 cans Italian Sauce (Tall size)
1 can Enchilada Sauce (10 oz.)

1 1g. Can Tomato Paste. Throw in few hot red peppers & Banana Peppers.

OPTIONAL: Fresh red tomatoes (chopped) to replace canned tomatoes.

½ Cup Chili Powder (Add more or less depends on your hot taste.

IMPORTANT! EACH TIME YOU POUR IN A CAN OR BOTTLE, ADD WATER AND SLOSH IT AROUND TO GET ALL AND POUR IN.

COOK!!! Stove top, bring all to slight boil tum heat to very low and simmer for two hours. Stir often. Don't let it stick. If you do you have to pour it into another pot and don't scrape any of the pot bottom.

Turn off heat. Let stand for at least an hour or more then simmer again for about another hour. IF YOU WANT BEANS ADD NOW, 5 LG. CANS KIDNEY BEANS OR PINTO BEANS. STIR IN AND SIMMER ANOTHER 40 MINUTES TO GET HOT.

You can leave out anything you don't like or add your own! Serve in bowls with shredded cheese on top.

GRANDMAS' LACE CORNBREAD

Over the years, that is mostly in the very deep past, Lace Cornbread was a special fast touch to the family meal. I remember Grandfather especially loved cornbread but lace cornbread was special. Part of what made it special there was such a shortage of food during the depression. People traded with one another for different items. He was a farmer and com was always at his table in many forms. He could trade it for sugar at the market or with someone for potatoes.

Meals were at home and the wives had to have it ready on time. Grandmother and Aunt Virgie would whip up what they called *LACE*

CORNBREAD. Sounded right fancy for something they had to quickly throw together because they had forgotten to make bread until the last minute.

Additionally, *LACE CORNBREAD* took very little cornmeal to create an abundant amount of satisfying bread. I can still see Grandfather reach for another piece as his dessert for supper. He'd grunt, "Better'n cake!"

THE RECIPE: LACE CORNBREAD

2 Cups Yellow Cornmeal (Plain) Use a stone ground, not fine texture.
1 ½ Tbs. Sugar
1 scant Teaspoon Salt
1/3 Cup Lard (Or Cooking Oil)
1 cup Cow Milk, (Add water to thin.)
Mix all ingredients except water. Stir well enough to make a thin batter, Batter needs to be very thin. Add water to thin.
In Iron frying pan, medium to large size, pour cooking oil, (today, I like Crisco). Bring to a nice heat for frying on medium high. With large spoon, scoop full and with circular motion pour slowly into pan. Do this with as many spoonfuls as will fill pan. Fry each on both sides to golden brown and loneness. Continue until all batter is cooked. The bread should look like old lace and will taste great. Like in the old days, it's very quick to make and different!

FIREHOUSE SLAW

2 Heads (Large) Shred fine
2 Large Carrots (Clean and shred fine)
½ Large Bell Pepper (Shred fine)
1 large shredded Onion (Keep onions in refrigerator and they won't make you cry!)

MIX ALL ABOVE IN LARGE MIXING BOWL. Set aside.

Add:
1 ½ Cups Dukes Mayonnaise (More can be added if desired for taste)
I Tbs. Olive Oil
2 Tbs. Mustard
1 Tsp. Salt (More if desired, but check later to taste)
2 Tbs. Black Pepper (Coarse Ground is good)
¼ Cup White Vinegar
3 Tbs. Water
2 Tbs. Sugar

Mix all together well. Add more Mayonnaise if you want more watery. Turn into serving bowl, cover well and refrigerate.

Slaw is best made ahead of use time, at least an hour. This is convenient for most meals. As well, slaw keeps well refrigerated tightly covered.

It goes great with hamburgers, hot dogs. *FIREHOUSE CHILLL* and is a great side dish for many other meals. Slaw is a great snack instead of cookies.

SALMON STEW FROM SEATTLE

2 Pounds fresh or frozen Salmon (Clean Skin, remove bones and dark streak under the skin)
Slice thin with sharp knife. Salt gently both sides and let rest 8 minutes.

½ Stick Butter
1 Onion (very small, chop very fine)
2 Tbs. Olive Oil
2 Tbs. Coarse ground Pepper
½ Cup Tomato Ketchup

1 ½ Cans Evaporated Milk
1 ½ Cups Water
1 Quart 2% Milk
In large Stew Pot (thick bottom), place Butter, Oil, Salmon and Onion. Bring to gentle simmer until SALMON is near done. (Only minutes, it will be a soft pink color. Don't stir! Immediately, remove from heat and add other ingredients except 2% Milk. Now stir gently to blend yet keep SALMON in pieces. Bring to a slight boil for about three minutes or so. NOW ADD THE OTHER MILK. Again, stir gently make hot without boiling. (Boiling curdles 2%Milk.)
Serve in soup bowls with any crackers or toasted French bread.

BAKED APPLE CHEESE PIE

8 Roma Apples (Clean, core and cut into large slices. Cover in bowl of water)
16 Oz. Grated Medium Cheddar Cheese
3 Tbs. Corn Starch
(1/3 cup Water) To mix together to pour over apples)
1 Cup Sugar,
½ Cup Brown Sugar,
½ Lemon Juice),
1 tsp. Nutmeg
½ Stick of Butter
I (one) can Crescent Rolls or Flaky Canned Biscuits
Grease bottom & sides of large pie pan or oblong baking dish. Place Crescents or separated flaky biscuits into bottom to make one pie crust. Push dough up sides for edge. Cut butter into thin pieces and spread over crust.
Remove apples from water and MIX OTHER ITEMS TOGETHER EXCEPT CHEESE. Pour into pie bottom and sprinkle cheese evenly over. Bake about 45 minutes at 415 degrees until bubbly and brown. SERVE!

PEANUT BUTTER PIE

CRUST:
1 ¼ cups Chocolate Cookie Crumbs (crush cookies in zip-loc with rolling pin).
¼ Cup Sugar
¼ Cup Peanut Butter Combine Crust ingredients and press evenly into 9" baking pie dish, bottom and sides Bake about 8 to 10 minutes at 350 degrees.

FILLING:
8 oz. Cream Cheese (Softened)
1 ½ Cups (Quality brand) Creamy Peanut Butter
1 Cup Sugar
1 Tbs. Soft Butter
1 Tsp. Vanilla Flavoring
1 Cup Heavy Whipping Cream (Cold)

Combine all FILLING INGREDIENTS except whipping cream and beat until smooth. Fold in cream (Not whipped). Spoon into cool crust then refrigerate.

Serve in small slices with a squirt of whipping cream.

CHAPTER ELEVEN

Time had passed since the last major fire. They were playing catch-up. Everyone had gear out re-cleaning to make it all spit shined. Trucks needed a real extra cleaning because of all the recent major use. At same time all was well inspected checking for breakage and any non-working areas on vehicles.

There had also been a bit of time since the Women in Fire Fighting had their famous *chili* party. Chief Jerry Thomas sat looking out the window of his office. He could hear a grumbling of an engine from a strange vehicle.

Suddenly, a throat cleared then a knock banged hard at his slightly open door. It was followed with a deep voice, "Here Chief! Sign here! There are seventeen of these certified letters!"

"Mercy! Exclaimed Thomas. "This is overwhelming! What the heck is going on?" He completed the signatures and walked the mailman to his parked scooter-car.

The fellow slipped into his seat by the open door. He grumbled as he found a few more letters. "Sorry, I had so many of these I missed a few! I wouldn't want to short you! It must be real important to need signatures. You'll have to sign these too!"

The man extended the additional mail with a pen.

"Thanks!" Smiled the handsome fire chief in his freshly dry cleaned uniform. He attended the final signatures and handed it back. "These are all job applications. Odd they came on the same day. Actually, we thought these would have been here before now. I'll bet you had them hidden somewhere so you could throw it on us at once!"

They laughed together.

"I wouldn't do you like that Chief! Maybe this will be real good. I read in the paper just yesterday there the City plans to give you some more people. God knows you fellows have a lot on your plate!" The mail carrier sympathized. "Seems like you have to constantly have help from other departments. That's what the paper said.

"That is true. We hope to get a new crew and another fire house too if we are lucky."

"Hope this will get you what you need. Government work is always slow in coming." The man added. "Well look over there! It's your Commander! Hey, Bailey! Are you back to work?"

Bailey snapped his head around, "Yeah, I expect this place is falling apart. I've been gone quite a while!"

"Welcome back, Commander!" Smiled the Chief as he gulped another whiff of the exhaust from the mail scooter. He waved good-by to the mail carrier. "Bailey, I need to talk with you. Come on in the station. Can you handle those crutches?"

"Certainly," snapped Commander. "I've learned it well. Your office or mine?"

"Yours will do!" Jerry replied. He knew it would be somewhat awkward for the man to have to go from one room to another.

The two men struggled to get into the smaller space. Commander winced as he puffed with the settling into his chair. He squalled, "Wheesh! Oh boy! It's a mess dealing with all this!"

"I can imagine so. Sooner or later it'll all be behind you and you'll be back in the drivers' seat."

"I hope!" Commanders eyes turned real red and tears dropped onto his white shirt. He snorted and made the effort to bring his emotions into control.

Anxious to return to business, Chief looked at his armload of mail and snickered, "Dig this!"

Quickly he flopped the load onto Commander Baileys' desk. He muttered and rolled his eyes, "What the devil is all that?"

The two pulled the string around the mail and it flowed gently across the desktop.

"Look them over, applications for firefighter. We have four important openings to fill as of this morning. There are several more forms on my desk. I'll get them for you. We can both read them and go over them together later.

"I hate hiring people! To be factual, I like to fire people! It's easier to dump a dog than to try to find a new critter!" Thomas chuckled as if he thought he were a comedian. Sadistic moods were part of his nature. He loved to have others as the brunt of his *jokes*. He thought it was a way to keep his comrades in line.

"Look, this is serious and vitally important. We are working almost one crew short. We barely have it covered even with adding overtime from some of our people. It isn't fair to our crews and not fair to the city. We must get this in check right away!" Chief looked into the man's red eyes and required, "Read! Read every one of these applications now!"

"Hold it a minute, Jerry! Who is being replaced?"

The Chief stopped and turned, "Nobody! We have all these candidates to research for new firefighters. We need to replace some for those who retired and they are allotting us extra people. For now, we hope for at least seven hires. I don't demand much of you but now I am. Read these and we can meet in the morning at 9:00 in the conference room!"

He accidentally slammed the door as he left, even so he heard the Commanders' remark, "The bastard, thinks he can give me the one, two, three! I'll pick the people I know. Who wants new idiots? They're all the same anyhow. Humph!"

Chief kept going and stuck his head into the kitchen where the crew was having their breakfast. Todd, when you're finished please come to my office."

"I'll do better than that, I'll bring you breakfast!"

Chief accepted, "Good, that will be great!"

Soon, the young fireman who was vital to Engine 27 Company strolled into the bosses' office. He was boasting a large breakfast tray full of everything that would cleanse the nerves of an aggravated man. Joe Todd placed it on the desk and handed Jerry a large white napkin.

"Boy do I need a good cup of Chock *Full Of Nuts*! You are the only one who knows how to make a real pot of coffee!"

"Hope that will be a bit of job security!" Thrilled Todd. "By the way, did you know the *wolf* is back? You know... the commander! Some of the fellows saw his car parked in his space. They said he's on crutches. Yes, Sir! He's back!"

"That's right, he's back in the flesh! I had the pleasure of seeing him already!" Chief informed. "In fact, I helped him to his office."

"Oh!" Todd gulped and poured them another cup of coffee. "Hear this!" Smiled the Fire Chief. "I received a stack of job applications from the women firefighters. Remember their Chili episode? Them! I simply handed the applications to him and demanded he read them all. Just wait until he catches on, all women apps."

The two lifted their cups and sighed with anticipation. The firehouse became strangely quiet except for the click of the distant clock.

Todd whispered as if in respect of the silence, "Oh, Lord! He didn't know about those women applying?"

"Nope!" Chief began flipping the additional applications in a stack on his desk, "We need to drop these to the Commander. I have already gone over these. Some good people have applied. Ultimately I will go over the others. Here, take these to him"

Todd departed and entered Bailey's office.

"Don't you knock?" He snorted then sniffed and stuffed an obvious bottle into a side drawer.

"I was trying to welcome you back! Maybe we should have sent you flowers and candy!" Todd tried to tease.

"Aw, shut up!" He grumped.

"Well excuse me! I am just trying to be friends."

"Friends? Have you taken leave of your brainless mind? What man here would be your friend you silly dilly. We all think you are a twerp!" Bailey laughed mockingly. "Mister Twerpy!"

"The Chief sent these to you." Todd tried to recover.

"Chief, hell, I'm your boss! You listen to me!" Commander ranted on, all but out of control.

Todd quickly became silent to only listen.

"Buster, I ain't forgot that you are the one that put me on crutches in the first place. You wait, Jerk, I am still going to recommend they run you out of the department. You might get a job in the sewer plant! They need to fire you now!"

He knocked a glass off the desk and continued.

"See all these people in these folders? They want your job! I look forward to see the day the City hangs you for your stupidity! That's between me and you!"

Slobber frothed down the sides of his mouth and he began punching Todd in the lower ribs with his index finger, "I'm taking action to have you suspended right away and then fired! I'll get you, old boy! I'll get you! There's not a thing you can do about it!"

"This is from the Chief!" Quickly Todd placed the forms on Baileys desk and raced from the office. He felt tears of anger swell up in his eyes.

"Get back here! I'm not done with you!" Bailey roared to no avail.

Todd kept going feeling like a fool in search of a safe place to hide and collect himself. Immediately, he felt another body against his fleeing form. "Oh! God!"

"Nope! I'm not God!" Della managed. "What are you doing?"

"Nothing!" sniffed the man feeling helpless.

"Not acceptable! What's going on?"

Todd broke, "The damn Commander! He's back! He hates me!"

"He hates the world!" She consoled. "You'd think he'd be decent after all he went through."

"Not him! I'm first on his list from hell. He blames me for his *idiotic* fall. He's going to get me, he said so!"

Della slid her arms around Todd and slid herself close to him as though he were a child to comfort. She whispered, "I'm here for you. Don't worry. Things will work out. I promise! I love you Todd!"

He looked into her soft eyes feeling something he had never anticipated. Tears drizzled down his cheeks. A burden seemed to have left him and a new picture was before him.

Mysteriously, their lips met. They found themselves deeply and tenderly exploring each other's mouth and tongue. Their body heat raged quickly as if a *five alarm* fire. They clung together as if there was no other world.

As fast as it all came about, they both quickly pulled away. They both knew the place was wrong. Nobody had ever put romance to the test before in the firehouse, not that they knew about.

Considering the risk, they both whispered, "I'm sorry!"

Yet, nearly out of breath, Todd and Della stood searching each other with continuing desire.

Although reality said "No!" Their hearts and bodies said, "Yes! Yes! Yes!"

Again they wrapped themselves together in a heated, steamy embrace with hot desire. Both thinking, *'It cannot happen here again!'*

Della reasoned need. He reasoned desire. They were trapped in love.

The loud blast called, *the bell* saved them! Now they were ON CALL and running to seek their place on Engine 27 as they were beaconed to duty.

The in-house speakers were announcing their plight. The whole crew whipped into the *turnout* gear placed by their duty spot next to the truck. Once all firefighters were aboard, the bay doors would noisily rise and they were on to immediate action. The driver gave a long blast of warning as he cautiously moved the huge vehicle to the edge of the road. As always he continued into the direction of the proposed event.

Della watched Todd in a jump seat from a mirror. He still seemed shook up. Her mind cast to the thought of the Commander and his *hissy-jit.* She squinted her eyes thinking, 'Ole Bailey is hell! He tries to crap on everyone. I'll just watch out for all of us, especially my poor baby Joe Todd. He is so wonderful!' She smiled as she remembered his hot lips and big strong arms around her.

The address for the call was immediately ahead of them. The driver expertly stopped the fire rig in front of the building. All firefighters rushed from their seats to organize the response.

Captain Williams swerved his car to park in front of the big red ladder truck.

FRIED GREEN TOMATOES

1 Jumbo egg
½ Cup Buttermilk
¼ Cup water
Combine and mix, set aside. In bowl, place together:
½ cup Flour
½ Cup White Cornmeal
Teaspoon Salt
Teaspoon Black Pepper
Set aside.
4 Medium size Green Tomatoes, Clean (Slice in 1/3 inch slices, place on thick paper towel)
2 to 3 cups Crisco (heat in iron skillet)

1. Lightly flour slices of tomatoes
2. Dip in Egg mixture
3. Dip in try mixture
4. Place in the hot oil skillet
5. Fry on both sides until golden
6. Place on paper towels or rack to drain. Sprinkle gently with salt.
7. Serve!

CHAPTER TWELVE

This call was a great relief from the station house and angry Commander. It cleared every one's mind.

Captain was calling commands, "Della, go find the person who called in the alarm. It was phoned into '911'."

"Sure, maybe there's a cat in a tree. I don't detect any smoke!" She replied then quickly found the entrance. The door was open. Motioning to the two firefighters behind her, they rushed inside.

A man behind the counter looked up in bewilderment and asked, "Can I help you?" He could see the emergency crew was there on business. He looked worried yet confused. "You ain't cops! You don't look like cops. Usually its cops that come."

"No, we're not the police, we are the firefighters." Informed one of the backups.

"Is there a problem here? Somebody phoned in. They reported this building is on fire!" Della boldly related.

As they talked to the man the two firefighters with Della began looking around the open room. One stirred into a trash-can placed too near a heater. The other guided his attention to the loose wires overhead. Both made mental notes regarding these situations.

The crew outside was ready to handle whatever the crisis might be. They expected the inside party to return with immediate directions.

"We ain't got no fire and we ain't called" he replied. "I'm sorry! I don't know *nuttin'* about it!"

"Somebody knows. They dialed 911 for help!" Insisted Della.

The fellow appeared aggravated, he cracked, "Here, take these matches and make yourself a fire if you want one so bad! We ain't called!"

"Is anyone else is here?" persisted Della.

"*Naw*, we just take care of these mailboxes." He looked more worried when a noise from a back room revealed additional movement and implying that he was lying.

"What's back there?" Inquired a fireman.

"*Nuttin*, might be the cat."

Della spoke into her communication device. "Captain, they proclaim nobody called. One man is in the front."

"I'll be there in a second!" Captain Williams knew she was perturbed and motioned to Todd with a nod of his head. "Come on! Let's see what's the score! We're wasting time."

As they entered the place, two men rushed toward them as if they were being chased.

"STOP!" Della commanded.

Instantly they heeded her order but were in the face of the men entering the doorway.

One fellow cried out, "We're leaving. We don't know anything."

Captain and Todd stood about a foot White with fear, the guys decided to talk.

One squirmed but looked away as he pretended to unload. "We *wuz* just gonna play a few hands of cards. We're higher than the two *short jerks*. Captain nudged one and asked, "Anything, what?" leaving now. Just a friendly game not bettin' or *nuttin'* like that."

"That's right!" agreed the other chap.

"Did either of you call in a fire alarm?" Snapped Captain.

Todd added, "If you did we'll find out. The phone system records everything. Believe me, false alarms don't go unpunished. We'll know, we always do!"

"None of us know about this. How many times do we have to say it! Ain't heard it, ain't seen it and ain't smelled it!" One rendered in fear.

The other one shook his head in agreement. "Ain't *nerry* fire!"

Captain Williams knew these were not the one he would be looking for. He stared intently studying their body language and tone of voice. He concluded although they may not be the caller something was happening at this address.

They were all he had for the moment so he'd push their buttons just a little more. "I see; then do you know who might like to see our trucks run?"

"Naw!" They chimed out together.

"Well, fine. I appreciate your cooperation. You two need to hang out here until the police arrive for farther inquiry." Captain wanted to smile as the two turned whiter.

"Oh, golly, can't we leave?" A bumpy faced fellow pleaded. "We just come here for cards, that's legal. Sometimes we bring a beer to drink with our buddies."

"Is this a private club of some sort?" Thomas Williams requested.

"I don't know; we just hang out here. They have mailboxes for people that don't have a place. Well, you know street people need this address. You can get your check in this place and other mail. We even get junk mail if we sign up and pay for the box. This is sort a like those U.P.S. Stores." He revealed.

He was satisfied with that bit of information.

Blue lights were flashing through the doorway. They could hear activity at the fire truck and doors slamming. The entrance fully opened to reveal a tall thin woman in a crisp uniform step her way to the Captain.

She reached for her notebook and pen to begin her investigation.

"This is for you, Officer. Apparently it's a false alarm. These fellows may have some input for you. We need to verify what these people really do here. They claim it's their mailroom, as they say *their U.P.S.* place. Probably something more is transpiring." Related Williams.

"What else?" The young cop asked.

"Someone called in an alarm and this is not the first time from here. We cannot be taking people and equipment on useless trips. It cost too much. Try to find the caller! "He smiled and whispered. "When you this finish run by the Station and fill me in. By the way, Gina Ballard is making *Rabbit Stew* for lunch. Her husband had a good hunt!"

She giggled, "Sounds great. I'll be there."

The crew returned to the truck. Everything had to be placed back to its place. Captain drove to the station in his car.

Finally, everything was accounted for and firefighters back in their seats. They turned the truck around in a nearby school parking lot and headed back to the station somewhat confused.

A firefighter was disturbed, "I'm sick of these false alarms. They're going to call and screw up something important. You can't be everywhere at once."

"Captain is going to get to the bottom of it. Just wait and see!" Della promised. "The police department is involved now. When fire bugs see the cops come, they usually stop but often they'll move to a different spot."

The bay doors were up and the big truck rolled in. They were just in time to hear the speaker announcing another Call. Without leaving the vehicle or totally stopping, the big wheels kept rolling on through. The driver listened carefully to the dispatcher and eased into the street with lights, whistles and horns going full blast.

Traffic around them pulled over to yield for them to pass. One truck would not be enough to handle this order. The call was sent out to the rest of the available fire trucks the city keeps in service. This event would soon place all of the them at a furniture factory.

Occasionally factory calls were quite minor. The crew would do and go and all extra units would return to their stations. Other fires were hectic and often very serious. They were very unpredictable, hot and difficult. When they would arrive there, the plan would be PAY CLOSE ATTENTION.

As Engine 27 noisily clattered its well-known route, everyone onboard was mentally preparing for the hazardous trip.

Again, Della fixed her eyes on Todd. He was seriously watching the route ahead. Color had returned to his face. She imagined that the earlier incident was just a freak happening and decided to leave it alone. She pondered to herself, 'If anyone knew we'd be fired... jobs would be gone.'

Slowly Todd turned to face her. He blushed and flashed her a wide smile revealing perfect pearl-like teeth. He shook his head approvingly and winked.

Della felt like a teenager and wanted to scream. Fortunately, the weight of the turnout clothes kept her down, she thought. Todd was such a handsome man.

Once more, the big rig jolted to a stop at a place where its occupants hated to go. This wouldn't be a small job. They could observe smoke rolling from the top part of the building near the *dust bins*, a very complicated and dangerous area.

"Let's get it!" Williams screamed.

All firefighters listened for their orders as they located the entrance. Williams ordered the Dalmatian back to guard the truck.

Promptly, they made their way to the top of the huge two-story building that is a portion of this mass collection of units that makes furniture for around the world. *The top of the factory had become the place for the dust bins.* They had to collect the dust and debris somewhere.

In various areas of the ongoing lay of buildings, big monster sized ductwork had been installed to force the waste materials to the collectors. Giant fans enabled them to get the task done with a flip of a switch and along the way other devices were added to enable the shavings and sawdust to be out of the way. This waste material would be sent into the dustbins. Then often as needed big tractor-trailers would roll in and receive a load. This waste was valuable in the fact that it was sold to another manufacturer for making chipboard, particleboard and other by-products.

Like many what seems routine situations, true safety goes unsecured. Even with fire drills, supervision and safety checks throughout the factory there was always something needing attention.

The most hazardous part of the dustbins was not easy to detect. When these big collectors began filling up they often would get hot spots that created major gases that could erupt for many reasons. Sometimes these bins would get very hot and smoke even start a fire.

The fire department was expected to handle this problem no matter what the cost. At times it was as if these extreme problems were considered a part of their life. The firefighters have been dispatched several times a day to check, look and listen. On every trip, the gut connects to that familiar sick feeling. This is not like regular fires but a major part of the cities safety. You have to always remember peoples' lives and the workers' safety are involved too.

It is all about the elements that are so intense to make dustbin activity every trip worry. This is unfortunately a feast or famine day this day. It all had to be strictly evaluated once on the roof.

Williams motioned for the crew to hold up. He expected to investigate and put into place one of the normal attack plans for this Call. He looked away for just a second to start Todd into his place.

Everyone's heart nearly stopped at the sound of a voice screaming.

"Come on!" Yelled Robert Timmons one of the newest firefighters. He was so excited with his discovery. "We have to hurry! There's a blue light!"

"Come back! Come back!" Williams panicked. "Back off! Now! Come back! It's ready to blow! Come..."

The rest of his words were lost.

The ambitious young firefighter had gotten to the upper hatch and touched the latch. As they all watched in shock, the firefighter apparently managed to let enough oxygen into the bin that was already like a deadly fuse.

Whatever happened, it was enough to set off a deafening blast that rocked the world around them. Parts of the building seemed to fly wildly into pieces while the blast roared its energy that made the whole area tremble as if an earthquake.

So often the collector fires give early notice to warn the employees. No matter who you are or what position you have in the business this was one to take serious, very serious. These people heeded the major warnings and rushed together in fire-drill fashion. They knew the sound that conveyed the story.

All possibilities of danger were in their minds and they were in grave fear for their lives and their jobs. Never before had they experienced such an ear shattering sound followed by the internal fire alert system and the showering from the overhead sprinkler system.

The activity everywhere was amazing. Everyone had to respond. The word spread fast. Without delay, every fire unit was *ON CALL*.

Each fiercely entering the fantastically overwhelming scene to do their part to assist with whatever would be needed.

Fire Chief Thomas formulated his command area and produced the immediate plan. Many lines were already in place and laying water in powerful force to knock out the first degree of danger.

The blast had showered live debris around that had to be captured immediately. The worse possible fear had shown its horrid head. Fire with death was nearly unbelievable and yet everyone had to carry on. They couldn't stop!

First responders kept their pace to duty and the additional fire crews worked their orders. The massive alarm had summoned all law-enforcement and medical teams who arrived to add their assistance. The police rushed to control the employees once they exited the plant and the medics had to face their role.

Many hours were involved to retain and elude farther risk to the decade old furniture house. It was tedious and dangerous and a sizzling effort in the 98-degree humid weather. Carry on, they must.

From the technical problems involved and the heat, several of the firefighters were sent to local hospitals. Exhaustion and minor injuries crowded the Emergency Room for help.

Many factory workers and firefighters suffered emotional trauma as well. It was a terrible fate to learn of the death of your work mate or friend. The buzz spread with all kinds of stories. Even so, right or wrong about details, the final word would still be the same, *ONE DEAD*!

Eventually, all had to turn around. Finally, with heavy hearts those left behind would have to clean up the situation to follow up the final orders.

How tough it is to be an on the top of the world, hero most of the time, but drop to the other end of the world in sadness. In the firefighting business, go and do is constant. Most of the time all is well, but this one... you still go and do.

"Todd, come here!" motioned Della. Her face was splotched with soot. "Oh gracious, hasn't this been unreal!"

"Yes! We were there!" He replied. "In training, this is what we spend lots of time studying. The warnings are there. You have to believe all of the warnings. They are there."

"I know!" She muttered and looked toward the sky. "Robert Timmons was a good person but too zestful. I had told the Commander to not let him loose yet. He needed to wait his full six months out."

"I said the same thing!" Todd remembered. "He was a great guy but needed more experience. I hate this for us all! Wow, this just doesn't seem right at all!"

Della tried to twist the subject to another page. "There have been so many Medic trips too, I hope there were no other bad injuries."

Todd smiled as tears developed in his eyes. He cleared his throat. "In spite of everything, the rest of us did great."

"Yes!" She acknowledged crying too. "We have to keep keeping on. The hardest part is I have never before seen the coroner pull the sheet over the face of another firefighter, someone I know! Robert was already gone; I know but this ruled him from life."

The two embraced quickly. The warmth from each other brought back the care they felt. For that, it should be a time to rejoice and smile. Life deals a trump card every now and then. Still having arms to hold onto in grief was so special.

Sadly, they walked back to their place on Engine 27. Together the whole crew had reinstated the big red rig to its working order. They had placed all tools, line and apparatus in the proper places. They were silent.

Chief Thomas watched his people as they gathered the implements. He could see the faces streaked with tears and their sadness giving away to heavy hearts. He knew well they too were trying to justify the death of a comrade.

It would be vital in the days to come that he help each one to understand there was nothing anyone could have done to reverse the situation. If anyone should take the blame, he thought it should be himself. Maybe he had neglected to get vital training points relayed to every firefighter.

Quickly he shrugged off the blame game. There would be no purpose served to guess or second-guess. It was done, no go back this time, it was done, happened and over. Forward with a new start was the only way.

He vowed to be a bigger shoulder for his people and face their needs fully. He would accept no more set-aside or waiting regarding the safety of his firefighters. It would be the main thrust of investigating to change the dust bin problems at these furniture establishments.

Back at the station, the atmosphere seemed weird. The place was buzzing with all the city officials, Mayor, City Manager, Council people along with wives and family of the firefighters. Nobody seemed to know what to say. Words were hard to find that wouldn't be empty. Just what can you say to the partners and loved-ones of a fallen fellow.

The News media now swarmed the station house. As the photo journalist encircled the returning fire engines for some kind of extra special photo. The crew dismounted and tried to avoid the photographers and the ready plea of questions.

Television crews worked diligently to seek out their intense storyline in the competitive rush. It was understandable and necessary to talk. Chief Jerry Thomas asked the Mayor to join him with the press. The public has a right to correct information. They needed to know about a death in a fire and the impact that the community would feel. They needed to have an understanding put forth in their hearts.

Chief Thomas looked directly into the many cameras and spoke softly.

"Robert Timmons was one of our newest firefighters. He bravely raced to the top of the factory and lost his life defending the challenge of a severe fire. We are still investigating this situation. We cannot guess with this sort of engagement.

Our hearts and love goes to his father, mother, brothers and family. He will be missed by all of us. Due to his sudden accident, the city plans to research how to correct the problems of firefighting around the dustbin. They are true disaster pits. While we are forced to mourn this young man and friend, Robert, we'll search for answers that before had not been recognized.

You will be notified of any further information."

As the department buzzed, the crew tried to find the refuge of their rooms.

RECIPES FROM THE FIREHOUSE

THE BIG SHEET CAKE

(Wonderful for birthdays and grand parties. Decorations optional!)
2 ½ Sticks Butter (Room Temp.)
3 1/2 Cups White Lilly Plain Flour
2 ¾ Cups Sugar
¾ Cup White Lilly Self-Rise Flour
3 Tablespoons Very Hot Water
3 Teaspoons Baking Powder
6 Eggs (Separate into two containers)

½ Cup Sour Cream
1 Tablespoon Vanilla Flavoring
1 ½ Cups Evaporated Milk
1 Tablespoon Almond Flavoring
½ Cup Water

Mixing directions:
Cream Butter and Sugar at low speed in mixing bowl for 8 minutes.
Add hot water and mix 2 minutes. Let sit for 5 minutes,
Beat egg yolks enough to not see color.
*Have all dry ingredients ready.
*Have all wet ingredients ready.
Slowly alternate stirring in dry and wet ingredients including flavorings.
Beat egg whites to a stiff peak and fold into batter.
*Have ready a 12X16X3 cake pan. Grease with Crisco and flour gently. Remove all excess flour.
Pour batter evenly into pan.
BAKE: 345 Degrees. (About 40 minutes or until done.)

Remove from oven and let cool about 8 minutes then dump quickly onto serving sheet or plate. Cover until completely cooled. When cold, cover with frosting and decorate as desired.

ICING FOR BASIC CAKE

3 Sticks Soft Butter {Let warm to room Temperature)
3 to 4 cups Confectioners' Sugar (Good Brand best)
Cream together by hand or small hand mixer.
Add: 1 egg and 1Tbs. Vanilla Extract, beat to spreading consistency.
Add drops of water if too thick; too thin add powdered sugar. Icing will thicken as it cools.
Refrigerate to set before spreading.

This basic Icing can be many flavors and colors, try your own style!
FOR CHOCOLATE:
1 Cup Chocolate Chips
2 Tbs. Crisco
3 Semi-sweet Chocolate Baking squares
¼ Cup Water
Place all in small bowl and microwave about a minute until all is melted and will stir together. Let cool and add into all or part of Icing.

THIS IS GREAT ICING. KEEP IT TIGHTLY COVERED IN THE REFRIGERATOR FOR QUICK USE.

The leftovers can be used on cupcakes or any cake. In fact, it is just great to keep on hand. By keeping extra icing, you are ready to finish any cake at any time. You can add favors or colors.

It sets up about 15 minutes in the refrigerator and then spread, add things you like. Split strawberries always make a cake fabulous and squirt a decoration of whipped cream.

Add lots of peanut butter to a small amount of this icing and thicken with powdered sugar and decorate.

Blueberries give a tasty touch.

The sheet cake is great plain or covered. Add your toys and candles! Be creative and it will bring much fun and many smiles.

Make two cakes and use as layers. This could be perfect for any birthday, holiday or special event!

CHAPTER THIRTEEN

For several days' people had gathered in and out of the firehouse paying their respect. A memorial to Robert Timmons had quickly been established. This foundation was geared to research, education and force change needed for dust bin safety.

As well, a bronze firefighter figure would be added to the town square to keep the memory of Robert Timmons and other failed firefighters in the hearts of the city.

Firefighter Timmons had been a National Guardsman not long returned from active military duty. In three months he would have been married to a beautiful girl, his high school sweetheart.

His family loved him and church was foremost in his life. With it all devotion to his work was vital.

The only possible place in the city that could accommodate the predicted crowd for this mans' funeral was the football stadium. The same soil where he had spent years as quarterback for his school football team.

Many persons remembered those days as they started to fill the seats in the huge place. Firefighters, emergency service crews, police, patrolmen and dignitaries from all over the city, county and state found their place there to mourn.

With neighboring Fire Departments running "in-house" fire coverage, all of Firefighter Timmons friends and comrades were able to attend the special ceremony of the sad occasion. It was heart wrenching to see his companions as they wept openly, pouring their hearts passion with the knowledge of his plight and the fact that "this could be me".

Friends, relatives, church goers and even strangers filled the massive number of rough bleachers. Once the people were into their places there was a long pause of silence. One could have heard a pin drop with anticipation. A slight breeze moved the American Flag gently. The sun poured beams of warmth that felt soothing. A bagpipe group was sadly mourning their way through an open passage from the top of the bleachers to the edge of the ball field.

One could feel a chill cover himself and no eyes were dry. All people clearly worshipped with their song, 'Amazing Grace'. When the bagpipes completed their mission the standing crowd silently sat back to their seats.

The school band followed with "America the beautiful" so the mess dressed uniformed firefighters, all special dignitary guest and immediate family could be seated in the formal special seating area. Once there, a church bell choir followed with the "National Anthem" that was amazingly perfect.

Then it was time for a series of speakers who rendered special moments to remember and honor the life of Firefighter Robert Timmons. It was a beautiful union that supported the city, firefighters, friends and family.

Finally, the young mans' minister stepped to the podium to give a brief but loving sermon. He was saying, "Robert was a very special young man with a tremendous rapport. He was a man of love for his family, his special lady, friends, his fire duties and God.

As a child his parents followed the word of God and kept him close to the church. Just last Sunday, as the family walked from our service down the sidewalk, I recall seeing Robert at the bottom of the steps turn and wave goodbye to me. He beamed a happy smile and for that instant, all was well."

The clergyman cleared his throat, shifted his robe then continued, "Its for certain, Robert was doing what he loved at the time when he left this world. That is the whole point of life, to live ready!

Every day can be the last one we have. There is no assurance of the next. You must keep in your heart God loves us. Life is at its fullest when you are ready, prepared and like all firefighters, you do live ON CALL!

"Although Robert is no longer with us, his spirit will go forth for its born purpose. We are born to grow and find a station in life. Robert found his station. Some people never do. Search your heart and find where you belong. May God bless and keep you as you go forth."

The crowd all came to their feet with silent prayer. As earlier planned, the children from the church had passed red, blue and white balloons to all the attending children. With a silent command from the Fire Chief they let go of the beautiful balloons. It was as if hundreds of spirits carried them into a gentle wind. Everyone watched them sweep higher and higher and nearly out of sight.

The Fire Chief motioned the audience to be seated and introduced the Mayor. He had known Robert since he was a child. He also told of how he had followed the careers of many of the firefighters, including Timmons. The Mayors words were of encouragement for his vast protective corps that was always there. He expelled his appreciation to all friends, family and foe. Then he concluded with, "Let me share a special poem that was written by the Firefighters' wife to be."

HAIL TO THE FIREFIGHTER

To answer the call,
These heroes may fall.
But less they rush
From a depth they must!
Reaching for hands in despair
With dedication they are there.
A time to know, A time for will,
A time to care,
No time to kill.
They live devoted,
Always for the cause.
A firefighter is quiet,
And a hero to all!

The bells may ring at any hour.
They hit the door with full power!
Determined speed at its best,

Not concerned with any less.
They race on to meet the fire.
Day and night they will be there!
Yet other times they just go on,
Encourage a child if faith is gone.
Stillness rages some awful flames,
When breath of forever never came.

The heartbeat is close enough
To rush the power to do their stuff.
Sometimes a spirit from within,
Tells the firefighter,
"It's time, again!"

The Mayor smiled, "I believe that is a great description of all our emergency people and we appreciate the firefighters for their knowledge and bravery. We hold you all to the highest mark and salute your bravery."

"Let's remember Firefighter Timmons as the man who did take that fateful and tragic step that will reach beyond today. We will change those dangerous dust- bins and vow never let another man fall there. One life is far too many." He continued, "There is never enough to say that can ever patch the heart of the grieving."

He continued, "We do want the family of friends that belong to Robert to know our hearts are with you now and always!" His voice broke and he covered his eyes as he shed tears of empathy.

Quickly he sat and motioned for the Chief to continue. Chief Thomas immediately replaced him. He cleared his throat and searched for words. It was as if his mind went blank, his lips tuned white and dry as he trembled.

Finally, he opened his mouth and forced words, "I join with all of you. Today is sorrow, but tomorrow we must carry on. We learn from our tears of pain and replace them knowing when the sun shines tomorrow we will be richer because of a new determination and a reminder that things will be better." He looked around the crowd, "May God bless each of you and touch your heart individually."

With no more to say, his National Guard Unit took the field. They swiftly followed the military protocol with trumpets properly blasting out the "Taps" and the finale was the twenty one-gun salute with seven guardsmen firing three shots each. The Bagpipe group followed them to the waiting fire engine covered with the American Flag. Pallbearers lifted the flag covered casket into place to ease it inside the massive vehicle.

Family cars were in place to follow. Close friends were allowed to join as they paraded from the stadium for a private graveside service.

It had been a tremendous ceremony that would be silently remembered. When the local firefighters returned to their station they had to quickly relieve the assisting crews from neighboring area fire departments.

They were barely able to say thank you when the bells went off. The announcement was made over the speakers directing them to their next assignment. With turnout gear on, each firefighter was in place. The big bay doors once more opened for the vast fire truck to scream its way to its beacon call. The truck had to slow to get through traffic lights.

RECIPE FROM THE FIRE HOUSE

BASIC PIE CRUST

2½ c. Plain Flour
½ Tsp. Salt
½ Cup (plus 1 Tbs.) Crisco solid
10 Tbs. Ice Water

Mix together dry ingredients into large mixing bowl. Hand sift.

Place in Crisco, and use fingers to slide together flour and Crisco until it becomes like little marbles. It will be slightly less white when well mixed.

Add Water, slowly to mix. MIX AS LITTLE AS POSSIBLE! But get all the mixture together. If needed add more water, just enough to hold together.

Dust hands with plain flour (extra and make into a ball.) Split big ball into 4 or 5 small balls. Each will make a crust. Cool for at least 15 min.

Flour surface & roll each dough ball ¼» thin. (It should be rolled and flipped over and over. It will be a flat crust. Place in greased pie pan, and flute edge. Make top from a ball, roll, cut strips or place on top (cut air holes). Finish as desired. (Dough can be frozen)

FRESH FRUIT PIE

Use Basic Pie dough for crust. You can use bought frozen crust too. Usually you will use a bottom crust and top crust or strips of crust dough.

Select fresh fruit. Not over ripe is best. Use Apples, peaches, blueberries, fig, rhubarb, etc. If in a hurry, canned fruits are good but drain them and do not handle much.

7 to 9 peaches, or similar fruit, (5 cups.) Bowl: Sprinkle in 1 cup sugar. Add: Juice ½ lemon., 1/4 Cinnamon or other spices.

Mix together: 1/3cup water

2 Tbs. Com Starch

 Stir into fruit to blend all together

1 Stick of butter

Dot bottom of pie shell with butter patties, pour infilling and dot butter chunks on top of fruit.

Cover with top crust and dot with rest of butter.

Bake fruit pies at 400-degree oven for 45 to 55 Minutes until done. Should be golden.

CHAPTER FOURTEEN

The crew continued to this first call since the vast funeral. It wasn't easy.

A car stopped in the middle lane. This took more time. Finally, they were in easy traffic to travel on to their destination that turned out to be an old hotel. It didn't seem to have a fire. They unloaded and prepared to search the situation. Captain Williams said, "This is the same place we went to a week ago. That was a false alarm!"

"They claim they have a mail room there," Della remembered.

"A bunch of drunks hang out here," Joe Todd added. "Let's check it carefully regardless."

" I hope we don't have a new firebug on our hands," Captain replied, "Go on Della, look around and I will talk to the person in charge here."

Everyone moved immediately into place. Williams banged on the locked door. It took a few minutes until a heavy woman wearing a thick bed spread looking robe and huge elephant bedroom shoes stuck her head out the door. "Yeah? What ja want?" she growled through a mouth full of food.

"We got a call for this address. Where's the fire?" Williams demanded.

"Done been here fer that one time before. We ain't got a far fer ya. Maybe somebody got a wrong place," she snickered.

"Look it's not funny. Do you know anything?" he sharply submitted. "This is serious not a game lady. If you know something say it now."

"Done told ya, ain't here! Just go on!" she chewed from something in her hand.

"We'll look around!" he advised her.

"No! Leave!" she screamed.

When he turned to go, someone hit him across the back with a broom. It was a wasted move.

The Captain swung around and grabbed the bushy stick from a young girl. He growled, "That does it!" From across the way he could see a couple of his crew observing the odd situation. It was embarrassing,

"Alright, get it checked out. Something is going on! That brat bashed me for no reason. I want to know if there is a fire here or who is playing a prank." The firefighters rushed around until they exhausted every effort.

No fire was found. It was a false alarm. Captain Williams rushed once more to speak with the woman who seemed to be in charge. When she returned she had put on jeans and a strange shirt. He wished for the sleepwear, it covered lots of ugly.

"Lady, here is a paper advising you this is a false alarm. It is your second in two weeks. If we are called on another false alarm, there will be a big investigation. I might even arrest that little brat for slamming me with the broom. You know I could." Williams rendered, "You had better find out who is making these calls. It cost the city about $5,000 for us to run out!"

"No shit Sherlock! That's your job. But I ain't called!"

"Alright, you've been warned," he said sternly. This time he backed away watching carefully. He heard her on the other side of the door cursing those in the household.

"You bastards, if you called that far department I'm in trouble. Who did it? Then you banged that big man in the back.!"

"He was being mean," whined a girl. "I ain't called them!"

Several other voices chimed in crying, "I ain't called."

The fire crew returned to their truck. On the way back to the station they discussed the odd call. Once the truck entered the bay, Captain Williams asked the firefighters to meet in his office for briefing. It was a short meeting about the strange event.

They read the current city ordinance regarding false alarms and were told to remember they have to still go on all calls, even suspicious alarms. It can be a real problem. These calls can come at the time of real fires.

Unfortunately, someone making false alarms is often a person with a mental quirk.

The day had been so wearing. It wasn't over yet. The public was still bringing food and leaning on their strength to help them with the story of the fallen firefighter.

Commander Bailey scuffled into the big kitchen and break room. He looked at the massive amounts of food. He snorted, "Why do people bring a corpse all this stuff? He's been dead for five days."

The others looked around at each other and lifted eyebrows. They didn't know how to talk to him. Obviously he didn't need to be consoled. "Todd, you eating some of this food? This is Timmons' food. I thought you'd be more upset. He was your buddy!"

Todd stood and dropped his paper plate into the trash. Several others followed. They went to another lounge away from the kitchen. Todd felt like a jerk and would like to have cried.

One Firefighter tapped him on his back and smiled, "Forget him! Bailey is a joke! He has to pick on us all the time. You did what everybody did. You haven't violated anything. People always eat at wakes and after funerals."

Della said, "Did you hear what the Commander said yesterday?" They shook their heads no. "He told the Mayor and Chief that Timmons died because he was stupid. He said he has been made into a hero that he isn't."

Todd looked up, "Are you serious?"

"Ask the Chief. It threw him for a loop. Old Commander is going nuts, I believe. He is sadistic picking on you. I don't see how you keep from knocking him out!" murmured Della.

"If I touched him on or off the job, I would be fired. That's what he wants." Todd reminded them. "He's our boss and he would love to get me gone from here!"

"Well, you aren't the only one he's after, you are just his favorite person to hate. You know he really does hate everything. It's worse when he can't get to his booze. That makes him ultra nuts. I thought after he fell out of the ceiling he'd be civil." Added another firefighter. "Can't we do something about this?"

"Not really, he'll retire in a few years or less," Todd proceeded with trying to compensate for the predicament.

"Maybe we can get a group signing with a statement about how he is," sighed Della. "A few years can be a long time. Not only that, it's stressful having to know he's on the wing. I catch him all the time sneaking up on people. He especially hates women in the department. Wait until they select the new recruits."

"He was boiling when the Chief made him read all of those applications from the gals. You know it will be interesting! They will be hiring about seven or so people." Reminded a Firefighter called Luke Storm. "I was transferred here until the others are hired, then I get to go back to station three. That's my home sweet home with no Commander Bailey."

"Shhhhhh! Shhhhh! Here he comes!" Della whispered and grabbed a magazine. The others quickly did the same thing.

"Well, what have we got here? Looks like the Fire Department Clan! Are there any new happenings I should know about?" He grumbled. "Bet you all wonder why I came tonight. I'll tell you. You know that false fire alarm you attended today? Did you not find out who set the alarm off?"

"It came in by phone not an alarm system. We couldn't track it." Luke injected. "It's hard to find out things in old neighborhoods as such."

"That's the difference in you young fellows and old codgers like me. I can sniff out this kind of nut." Commander bragged. "Get your gear. We will go back and do some checking. Williams can stay here at the station and baby sit the public. We will finish the job."

They looked at each other in amazement but placed their magazines in the holder and stood.

"We have to take the truck in case we have a call," he stated. "Todd you drive." As they readied everything for the trip, Chief Thomas rushed into the bay where the crew was getting into their turnout gear.

"Did I hear an alarm or are we running silent these days?' asked the Chief.

Immediately Captain Williams joined the Chief. He cocked his head and listened.

Todd spoke up. "Commander is going to take us to learn how to catch a fire bug. He says he'll sniff them out! We are going to that place we went to today."

"There's no need for that now," pronounced the Chief, "Put up your gear and relax. Bailey come into my office right away!"

The group watched the Commander quietly follow the Chief. Once they were safely out of hearing distance Della giggled, "His tail is between his legs! I'm glad Chief came in when he did. Want to bet something? When the Chief leaves and everybody is gone he'll make us drag out the tooth brushes and clean the floor for half the night."

"I'm not doing it ever again. He can stop that controlling crap. I've been through enough today that I will not take any humiliation and harassment from the jerk!" Todd retaliated. "Enough is enough!"

"How do you think you'll stop him?" asked a firefighter.

"I will get the Chief to come and stop it if I have to call his house." Todd had a new look about himself. "It's always something with him. I've had enough and the Chief can stop covering for the drunk. The commander is going to get somebody killed with his crazy demands."

Once more the fire bells alarmed throughout the building. Instantly they put all their troubles aside and raced to their station. The speaker started with directions and the driver started the engine of Engine 27. Each firefighter was seat belted in place and the doors raised to let them rush to *The Call*. Della caught a glimpse of Todd in her mirror. He looked back at her longingly. She sneaked a little wink and smiled.

The truck stopped suddenly near a railroad crossing. A car had stalled on the tracks. This was not *The Call* but something needed to be done. The driver called the station as Todd and Della lunged from the cab.

The two firefighters raced to the black Lincoln and jerked the front door open. A woman was slumped over the steering wheel.

"She's out of it! Call for back up and an ambulance. Tell the station we have another call here!" Della urged, "Todd, move her now! I hear a train. Tell the station to alert the trains we have an emergency!"

Another firefighter had followed them and ran to notify the truck crew of the situation. You could hear another fire truck responding to

The Call while Della and Todd assessed the vehicle in danger. The car was not running. Della tried to start it to no avail.

Todd had already rushed the lady out of danger. He placed her across the street. A policeman on foot patrol took over so Todd could join Della.

Once more they heard the train blowing its horn from down the track. Della had spotted two children with a dog in a case in the back seat.

When Todd returned she screamed, "Grab a child. The back doors won't open. Please, the car won't start. Hurry, I've got this one." Seat belts were hooked into place making it difficult. They prayed they didn't have to have the motor running to get them freed. The snapping of straps was good news and the pair was able to grasp the children securely.

They both jumped over the front seats to exit with the babies. The dog in the fuzzy box began to bark and whimper. Della stopped and snatched the handle of the case quickly. It was loose and was awkwardly beside her. "Todd, Grab this!" She squalled. "It's a dog!"

Todd obeyed and yelled. "Hurry! There's no time! That train is almost here!"

Della held the child to her chest tightly as she finished leaving the car. The train was almost there. She could see the face of the huge black and yellow engine rapidly roaring toward them with a deep horn blasting a warning over and over and over.

The oily tracks were hard to maneuver on foot but she managed to get to the edge. She saw Todd motioning her to come on.

The train horn kept blasting and she could hear a screaming of metal with tremendous air brake action as she threw the child ahead of herself in the direction of Todd.

Della was airborne herself as she lunged with all her might to clear the tracks. Falling into a deep ditch beside the track she hoped she was still alive. Her firefighter gear absorbed part of the impact, even so, she blacked out and lay motionless.

The train was trying to stop, from the warning message that had been dispatched to them. A train cannot stop on a dime. It takes a long time to force a rolling freighter to stop for anything. It had reduced the speed a little but still stormed through the intersection pushing the fine Lincoln down the tracks with pieces of the car flying all over the area.

Once the big monster shrieked to a final stop, everyone stared in disbelief. People were on divided sides of the tracks. Engine 27 and part of the crew had been marooned on the one side while the rest of the crew was on the other where the human rescue had taken place.

Todd and the police gave the babies to the EMT attending the mother. Soon they took them all to the nearby hospital.

The dog in the case was with a lady who had offered help. Todd rushed to Della as she began to move, "Hey, Girl, why are you hanging out in this ditch?"

"Oh, I hurt everywhere! I can't move my leg!" Della groaned. "Did everybody make it?"

"Thanks to you, everybody made it! You're my hero of the day." Todd motioned to the waiting EMT and held her close in his arms. He felt her nestle to his chest. Tears came to his eyes as he remembered her as a wonderful woman he loved. "Della, I can't help it, I love you. Oh mercy how close I came to loosing you."

Della felt a couple hot tears fall on her face. She looked into the sweet handsome man's eyes. It was fear and love and relief.

She whispered, "Todd I love you too! Just be quiet and hold me while you can. I'll be alright, we will be alright."

The medical team gathered her onto a gurney and slid her into a waiting emergency vehicle.

Todd watched her disappear from sight. Once more he remembered seeing her fly through the air as he revealed their rescue to the investigating police officer.

He told how the car was on the tracks and they had to get the driver out to try to start it. He believed it was out of gas so next best was to get the kids and dog. Everyone did what could be done and what seemed right.

"There are no rules on getting out of the way of a train. When a train seems a long way down the track, he is moving so fast that the speed puts him on you before you know it. The driver of the car is lucky you had that fire call." Smiled the cop. "That woman firefighter really pulled it off. She had enough time to clear out but had she fallen she'd never have made it. I saw her go into the ditch."

"Della is the best and tough." Firefighter Joe Todd admitted. "We might be in hot water for stopping. We were on our way to a CALL and obligated to get that one. Over there, over here, how do you call it?"

He added, "Another truck was right behind us. Once we bailed out, our crew notified the them. They took another route and went on to the other *Call*. I really don't know where I am. This train is here and my crew is on the other side. Can you call the station for me? Guess me and that other fireman over there are AWOL."

The policeman called and transferred the message for him. "Your Chief is on his way here. That's right cool!"

"I hope it's cool, sometimes it could be hot!" smiled Todd. "Chief Thomas is the best boss ever. We have a Commander who is something else. Can you find out if the train is going to move? We could walk to the other side."

"Not yet, but you can bet this train won't go anywhere for a while. They will have to clear the track in front of him. That car is all over the place. Even though the car is at fault, they still investigate. The media will have to get their thing too." Policeman added. "There's your Chiefs car now!"

Todd motioned the other firefighter on his side of the track to go to the Chief who was now standing beside his car. He rushed to join him. "I can't let you out of my sight and you find trouble!" he teased. "What a strange thing! You and Della are something else. How did you know that car was stalled?"

"It wasn't moving," he teased back. "I was seeing it in place as we were coming to it. It just didn't look right. We barely got the lady, two babies and a dog out. That train was rolling I will tell you. It seemed like a long way off and then it was there. Della had to jump out of the way! She is at the hospital now."

RECIPES FROM THE FIREHOUSE

EAGLE BRAND DESERTS

Four of the best simple deserts in the world are the recipes on the can of Eagle Brand Condensed Milk. Purchase four cans immediately and prepare them to the recipe. Each recipe is easy to make and you will become a hero to all!

I have made them all with never fail results. The best Fudge, great Cookie Bars, Marvelous Cheesecake and Perfect pumpkin pie. These are quick and delicious.

BREAD PUDDING

8 C. diced loaf bread
3 C. Milk
2 c. Sugar
4 Eggs
1 Stk. Butter (melted)
¼ teas. Vanilla
½ C. Raisins
¼ tea. Nutmeg
½ C. flowered nuts
¼ tea. Cinnamon
Mix all ingredients lightly. Place in (Buttered) Oblong pan.
Bake at 335F for approximately 45 to 55 minutes. Let cool slightly before serving.

CHAPTER FIFTEEN

The Chief had so much on his mind with another near tragedy involving his number one crew. The big train could have been five minutes earlier and killed half of them. Sometimes, he thought it was a handicap to be so observant. Then, that is what made this crew so amazing.

"Get in the car, we'll go to the hospital. He said. Once in the car Thomas continued. "That other fire call you were sent on was another false alarm. It was at the same place you went earlier. I have a meeting with the Police Chief tomorrow to discuss it. Somebody wants to play a nasty game."

At the hospital they learned the car driver was recovered but had a panic attack when her car stalled and lost consciousness. The babies were good to go and the puppy had been left in the emergency room.

"That was one happy ending although her car is gone." Todd joked, "Guess she will have to get Johnny Cash to put it back together 'one piece at a time' or get another one."

"I can see that now! Where is Della, you know our woman firefighter?" asked the Chief to the ER nurse who looked up. Her gorgeous red hair sparkled under the lights.

"You mean the woman from the train accident? She's in surgery. You can wait, but she will be there for some time."

"Some time?" Chief and Todd blurted out together. "No!"

"I'm very sorry. She is serious. They have tests and are doing everything for her. You need to call her family. She asked for you though." Replied the nurse.

Todd sat down on a bench, "I can't believe it, Chief. She said her leg hurt. Yeah, she said she hurt all over. She has to be alright."

"You stay here and wait for her family. I'll have the station to call. Pull yourself together. You can't go to pieces over your partner. She'll be fine. This is the best hospital around. That was a tough jump she made. She made it. I'll take care of everything at headquarters." Chief Thomas nodded to the other man.

It seemed forever before anybody came to the ER waiting room to talk to Todd.

Finally, the red haired nurse rescued him, "Sir, come with me."

He jumped quickly, "Is there any news yet. I mean something different?"

"It's too early. They assigned her a room upstairs and you can wait there. I ordered you some coffee and a sandwich. Eat it all. You'll need it. They have a long way to go with her. She'll go into recovery after surgery. We need to be able to have her loved ones comfortable and ready for her."

"Ready?"

"Alright, I'll tell you. Her right leg was shattered."

"I don't understand. Does that mean she'll loose her leg?" His mouth went dry and lips would hardly move. "Oh no, God, please!"

"The doctors are working hard. They hope to save it. Just pray." She said. "She has the best medical team. It all depends on what they find. Anything can happen. She will be a long time up there."

Todd felt numb. He tried to think while he searched for the assigned room. He said aloud, "This can't happen, not to tough ole Della. It can't be true. Della would never have expected to lose a leg. Even if she does, I will never leave her."

Todd called Chief Thomas at home and relayed the possible verdict.

Chief said, "Look, don't tell anyone else. Let's wait for her to get out of surgery. Maybe it will change. Not a word to anyone. A news reporter is on the way. Tell them nothing. Call me when she's able to see us."

"I'm supposed to be on duty!" Todd revealed as if surprised with himself.

"You went through a lot rescuing the people from that car. Do you think you're Superman? Maybe you should get yourself checked out!"

exclaimed Thomas. "Your duty was over hours ago. The Station house is set for now and you are where I need you. By the way, I'm going to recommend a special merit for both you and Della. You both need to be moved into new jobs. You both have certainly gone to the very edge. For now, just hold your drawers for me."

"I'll be here. Someone is coming now; I need to go. Its family I think." They both left the phone in near shock. Her condition was sadly fragile.

A tall woman who looked much like Della stood beside him. She looked down for a minute then uttered, "Where is Della?"

"Still with the doctors I suppose. They said it would be a long wait. She has to go through surgery, recovery and all that."

"I see. You must be Todd, her partner." The woman smiled nervously.

"I am. We had a rough day before the train incident. You know she saved lives this evening." Then he revealed the ordeal they had been through taking her up to the moment.

He learned this was Della's mother. He found it odd that she had never been to any of the fire department events where they could have met. Then, many families don't get involved. Some families just can't get into understanding the need of being supportive.

Time passed slowly and they sat awkwardly together trying to cope with the wait. Todd chose not to talk about Della. He wanted someone else to tell the mother of her daughters' total condition. That nurse might have told him too much anyhow.

"I'm going to the Chapel; do you want to come?" he whispered. The woman shook her head and watched the firefighter in the heavy turnout suit step from the room. His footsteps echoed on the waxed hallway floor as he walked away.

Opening the Chapel door was comforting. Todd sought a place on the front row just below a large candlelit cross. He bowed his head and tears surged into his eyes and he prayed aloud.

"Oh, Father, it seems like I have to come to you when I am in trouble or need a favor. This time it's about Della. You already know. You know all about our needs. I want to talk to you about Della.

Please, God, have mercy and let the doctors fix her leg. It would be so hard for her to lose it. She was trying to save people when she was hurt.

Please reward her if it's your will that you can help her come through a whole being. I promise to be there for her regardless. Thank you! Amen."

The door to the chapel opened. Several more people sat near him. Todd could see Dellas' family as he left the soft velvet clad room. He said nothing and returned to wait for her in the appointed room.

A woman in a blue uniform walked in with another pot of coffee and some ready sandwiches for those in waiting. She placed it on the long table with the first order. "I thought you needed a fresh-up before I go off duty. I believe they have sent her to recovery now. Did you see the doctor?"

"Oh no, I just returned from the Chapel," smiled Todd feeling tired for the first time. Afraid to ask for information, he studied her face for answers.

A familiar man in a white coat over a green suit noisily rushed in. He seemed upbeat at least. He asked, "Is the rest of the family here?"

At the moment the people returned. Everyone sat and waited. "The surgery is over. We will need to keep her in isolation and intensive care for now. She is still under sedation but we will have her awake soon." The man spoke.

"How is she? She will be alright, won't she?" Blurted out the mother.

"If all goes as we plan, she will be better than ever. I had two other surgeons assisting who are the very best and they have put her leg back together and if all goes right the leg will be good as new. We have to take every care to prevent any infection. With grafts and pins and many miracles she can recover well. Please understand she is going to be heavily sedated and need rest and your prayer."

The room was buzzing with somewhat relief and praise. They all knew the days ahead would be very trying and difficult. The mother hugged Todd in gratitude and cried.

Todd phoned the Fire Chief with the news. He sat down after his phone call. All of the trying moments seemed to pass before him. He closed his eyes and felt the hot tears stream down his cheeks.

He thought, 'Oh my special friend and partner, I want to be here for you always. Most of all, God has given you this break. You can come back as you have always been. Della, you saved those kids. Had it not been for you, we would never have entered that car. They would all have died. Oh, thank God for you.'

The shadows on the wall reflected a cross that was shining across the way. It seemed as if the angels were telling them all was well.

RECIPES FROM THE FIREHOUSE

CHIEFS PEANUT BUTTER MUFFINS

2 Cups Plain flour
3 Tbs. Baking Powder Dash salt
1/2 Cup Sugar Page 115
2 Tbs. Margarine (melted)
1/4 Cup Peanut Butter
1 Egg (beaten)
1 Cup Milk

Mix and sift all dry ingredients. Rub in Peanut butter with fingers. Add egg and milk then beat well. Stir in margarine. Have prepared a muffin pan that is well greased with Pam or Margarine. Spoon batter into the cups and bake in 400 to 425-degree oven, about 20 minutes or until golden.

CRANBERRY NUT BREAD

2 Cups Plain Flour
1 Cup Sugar
2 tsp. Baking Powder
1/2 tsp. salt
1 Jumbo Egg, beaten
A Cup Crisco
1 Cup Orange juice,
1 Tbsp. Grated Orange Rind
1/2 Cup chopped nuts,

2 Cups Coarse Chopped Cranberries Sift together dry ingredients. Cut in shortening until mixture looks like cornmeal. Combine juice and rind then add egg. Pour all into dry ingredients and mix enough to dampen. Fold in cranberries and nuts. Spoon into greased loaf pan. Bake 1 hour at 335 degrees (preheat oven).

This recipe can have a few versions. You can substitute the cranberries for raisons or figs. You can add another egg and substitute canned pumpkin plus another 1/2 cup of brown sugar. If you like a bit of nutmeg, sprinkle in a smidge of it. You can put this batter into muffin tins or small loaf pans to use as a gift. Touch the top with a shake of sugar.

DELLAS BANANA PUDDING

1 1/2 TO 2 Boxes Sugar cookies or Graham Crackers

6 to 7 pounds fine Bananas

Place in large bowl by alternating layers of cookies then bananas about 6 layers high. Use enough to fill the bowl but don't pack too tight.

Make Pudding: 3 Medium Eggs 1 can Evaporated Milk (Low fat is good) 1/2 can (from the milk) water, 1 1/2 Cups Sugar 2 1/2 Tbs. Com Starch 1 Teas. Vanilla Flavoring, 1 Teas. Almond Flavoring 1 Stick Butter (slightly melted) Place Eggs, Milk, water and sugar in top of double boiler. Beat to dissolve the sugar.

ADD: Com Starch and flavorings. Stir in butter.

NOTE: Bring water to boil in bottom of boiler for cooking. With Pudding in top of boiler bring to boil and stir often.

Once to boiling, stir continually or beat slowly. Don't let it stick or boil over. If needed, slow heat a bit.

When pudding thickens (and not too much), pour over bowl of cookies and bananas and help it to slide all the way to bottom. Use a knife to ease it downward if needed.

NOTE: This is a great pudding and can be used with other fruits or plain.

It can be place in individual serving cups and cooled.

Also, great with coconut and poured in a graham cracker pie shell. Top with cool whip and serve!

SAFETY TIPS FOR THE KITCHEN

Always keep cooking towels, dish clothes, paper towels, napkins, and loose debris away from the burners and flames on the top of the stove.

Never leave any flammable items on top of the stove when not in use. Accidents and carelessness cause fires.

Don't leave anything cooking when no one is around to attend it. BE SAFE AND RESPONSIBLE.

Keep floors and walk ways free of debris and can create many problems.

Fire Extinguishers need to be present where needed, especially the kitchen.

Drop cords can create hazards. Never buy cheap cords. Read about any cords when you purchase them. Heavy duty cords are best and usable for multi-use.

(NOTE: THIN CORDS SHIPPED HERE TO FLEA MARKETS AND DISCOUNTERS OFTEN HAVE SMALL HOLES IN THEM THAT CAUSE FIRES OR SHOCK.)

CHAPTER SIXTEEN

Some months passed before Della returned to the firehouse and all seemed in order. She along with several other firefighters had received promotions.

New people had been hired to meet the needs of the city and two more crews had been appointed.

Della had been concerned whether she'd remain with the old crew. They were so close and able to just seemingly read each other. On her first day back, she was met with a welcome sign and a breakfast festival in her honor.

Everyone was there along with family, many of the rest of the fire department and city officials. They now celebrate her return.

"Thank you!" Della sniffed with a big happy smile. "It's so good to be 'home' here!"

Chief Thomas held his coffee high and led the group with, "She's a jolly good fellow!"

Everyone joined in showing affection and happiness for her full recovery and return. Todd slipped beside Della, "Like this party?"

"You know it! Seems as if nothing has changed!" The woman replied. "I'm the party animal that invented parties!"

The two still had to keep their romance on a low key. You couldn't flaunt such in the work place. In the past others didn't have this situation. That subject had not been addressed. They both felt soon the shoe would drop. For now, they would let it rest.

Everyone gathered around with happy smiles to welcome her.

In time, everyone left the firehouse other than her crew and one additional young firefighter whom she had lots of influence with her hire.

"Ellen, you made our crew! Nobody even told me! We are lucky to have another person! When did you start?"

"Today! I was doing office things before now. The city has hired about thirty people. I know things will get better for all of us. They have the new station ready too."

"I have watched that go into place. How great it is to have extended area coverage. Todd and the media kept me informed. I don't know all the details. Probably won't be totally final for a while. I expect we will have to see how it all fits." Explained Della.

She smiled, "I guess you are ready to settle in. Captain will have someone show you the work routine and I will help you find your living quarters. It's so great that we have our own rooms here. There was a time that we shared a huge barracks type room and we shared snoring too!"

"I'm thrilled to have this job. Lots of departments won't hire women. They create reasons."

"There are laws that state the guide lines regarding personnel. We are most lucky to have such a great place to be and that we really are appreciated for who we are and what we can do." Della smiled, "Just be worthy. Only you can earn your respect and place."

"Believe me, I plan to do everything to go as far as possible. At least I have you to follow. I have always admired how you do things. I might make a lot of mistakes, but I hope that I don't repeat them." Ellen stated. She looked very pretty with her new shorter cut hair and her uniform fit neatly. "Todd gave me turn out gear last week. It all fits right."

"That is vital for you. I'll look at it too. We need to place it by our truck so when the *Calls* come in you're ready."

"I know. Todd assigned me a spot." She smiled sincerely. "It's in place already!"

"How about your place on the rig?" Della continued. "Yes, he showed me my seat!" "Super! This is so easy. You're already one of us!"

The two firefighters started toward the bedroom area but froze in their tracks with the first sound of the loud buzzers signaling them to their truck.

Along with the rest of the firefighters, they raced to their turn-out gear, dressed and quickly placed themselves on the ng.

The driver started the loud engine, and listened for directions as the big bay doors rolled up. Sirens were blasting and horns warning that they were underway.

Roaring into the street, they turned right and aimed for a gated housing area not far away. Everyone was listening to the commands coming through the system.

"Bet somebody cut a tree onto a power line near a house!" A Firefighter yelled. "May be somebody is hurt. See if they have EMT coming too!"

"I don't hear their siren" Ellen added.

As they pondered the plight, the huge truck soon stopped at the correct location. The air brakes announced their arrival with a dynamic loud hiss.

A young woman followed by a young girl raced out of the house toward them. She was waving frantically with tears in her eyes, "Come, let me show you where he is!"

Captain Williams followed her, "Come on! Todd, check dispatch and see if EMT is on the way!"

The crew followed to the back of the house but nothing seemed out of order. They looked all around, still nothing.

"Miss, what is the problem? I don't see smoke. Everything appears alright!" Williams winced trying not to lose his cool.

With huge tears and badly smudged make-up the woman, pointed and blurted out, "See him up there? It's our cat, Tarzan! We can't get him down!'

Immediately, she and the little girl began hysterically crying as they hung onto each other as if the world was totally over!

"Oh, God! Please let this truck full of fire people save Tarzan!" Loudly prayed the little girl.

"I'll have to call the firehouse," insisted Williams. "We'll try to do something!"

The woman and child stared as if they had been drugged, "Do it now!" They said together.

"Give me a minute!" Captain smiled as he turned to get his phone. While he connected with the Chief, he walked out of their hearing distance and talked quietly.

"Chief, we are at this house where we were sent. Dig this! It is a Cat in the top of a big oak. I mean the very top!

Tree is forty feet or so... "

Chief was laughing, "No kidding!

Do something!"

"Yeah, that's what she said!"

"You don't have anything else to do right now do you?" Chief roared happily. "Didn't you go to the tree and call, KITTY, KITTY KITTY! That's first! Give it to Ellen. She'll have the right touch!"

"So do this? Try to get the cat!" "Oh yes, this is a time to become a hero. We'll send a cherry picker and the news media. See you later!" He hung up.

Captain gathered his group in a huddle, "Chief says get him down! He's laughing at us too. Ellen, go over to that tree and call the thing. You know how to call one. His name is what?"

Ellen licked her lips, "Sure! I'm an expert! Watch this!"

When they walked beneath the tree, the big black and white cat scampered to the edge of the limb and started hissing and growling.

Ellen took her spot beneath him to coax the fellow out, "KITTY, KITTY, KITTY, come on down precious! KITTY, KITTY, TARZAN! Come on KITTY!"

The new firefighter kept on for quite a while and the cat just stared with his big green eyes. He seemed to be enjoying being out on a limb while everyone below patiently waited.

Ellen continued calling Tarzan for a very long time.

"Mee-ow!" The big cat would growl, hiss and call back as if mocking Ellen.

"He's not coming. He is probably just scared and afraid to come down!" Ellen decided. "I guess we'll have to go after him!"

"Oh, please go after him!" cried the child once more becoming tearful and concerned. "I can't live without Tarzan! He is everything to me!"

"Let me keep calling, maybe he will decide to come on. After all, he does have climbing gear." She advised. "It's silly to let him get it over on us."

The woman changed her strategy and went to the bottom of the tree. The cat watched and moved back toward the trunk.

"See, he's getting ready to come down, Come on KITTY... KITTY... KITTY! Come on and we'll give you some tuna and milk! Here, Kitty...Kitty...Kitty!

One of the firefighters observed, "He is not coming! Besides, you don't eat tuna with milk!"

The crew laughed in a teasing manner.

"Keep calling. Look, that jackass has gone up the tree farther! What an idiot!"

The little girl began to cry, "Tarzan is not idiot! He is a good boy!"

Finally, Captain suggested the mother and daughter go into their house and let them handle it. They agreed.

Ellen kept begging and talking to the creature in hopes it would come down. This went on for a couple hours until the city finally sent the cherry picker from the lighting department.

The driver smiled, "I should have known, cat in a tree! Who is going for the ride?"

Ellen stepped up, "I guess this is my real bucket list. We have tried doing everything."

"That cat is really angry. Listen to him! I have never seen one so mean. Be careful that he doesn't scratch or bite you!" The worker reminded her.

The woman got into the bucket and held on for the big lift. The man slowly and gently eased the bucket into place and aimed toward the place in the tree where the mad cat was perched.

Ellen continued to talk to the little beast with high-pitched sweet words that should entice a mushy baby kitten.

Tarzan stared and groaned and occasionally screamed that death roar he had developed.

Ellen's heart pounded with fear and uncertainty. Even so, she had to prove herself now. It was Tarzan or Ellen! She closed her eyes as she reluctantly reached out and whispered, "Here Kitty!"

Nothing happened. "KITTY, come to Ellen!" Again nothing. The awful growling and hissing stopped. Ellen peeped through her eyelashes. The big cat stared at her and flipped his long tail.

Suddenly, he turned and raced down the tree and rushed through the 'cat door' of the house. They heard the little girl scream, "Tarzan! You are safe!"

The fire crew and the gathered crowd began to clap as Ellen removed herself from the picker bucket feeling stupid. "At least that hateful cat is home again!"

The news media had gathered around to send a story to the city that there was a happy ending. The T.V. reporter summed it up, "It took seventeen people to bring the Kitty home. Most of all, this fire department is always there to assist our citizens."

They laughed to ether and returned to the firehouse. Ellen knew it would take a long time to live this down.

Later, after everyone had gone to bed, Ellen was startled and heard whispering. Then, voices together, "Here, KITTY, KITTY, KITTY!"

All lights turned off while the teasing laugh ceased.

The screaming warning and buzzers called out in the dead of night at four ten. Once more, they were *ON CALL!*

RECIPES FROM THE FIREHOUSE

DAVID'S PUMPKIN SPICE CAKE

1 ½ stick Butter (room temp.)
½ tsp. Salt
1 ½ cups Sugar

<u>Blend together for 8 minutes.</u>

ADD: 6 X-large Eggs (Wash to clean eggs) Beat in above mixture, one at a time.
STIR IN:
1 ½ tsp. Cinnamon
1 ¼ tsp. Nutmeg
½ tsp. Allspice
*optional: 1 tsp. Pumpkin Spice (Any spice could be left out if desired.)
Place together:
1 ¼ cup Plain flour
½ cup Self-rising Flour
pkg. Spice Cake Mix (or Butter Pecan)
1 can (15oz. Pumpkin (or your own cooked pumpkin in the same amount)
Blend all together and put into pans. This works well in flat pans, loaf pans or cupcakes.
Bake at 350 degrees according to pans.

TWENTY-FIVE CENT CUP CAKE

½ C. Crisco shortening
1 C. Granulated Sugar
2 ½ Baking Powder
¼ tsp. Salt
Cups Plain Flour (or cake flour)
1 Egg (Jumbo)
1 Cup Evap. milk (Using part water.)
1 tsp. Vanilla Flavor
½ tsp. Almond Flavor
Mix sugar and Crisco about 6 min.
Add egg, blend.
Combine dry ingredients, place half into first mix.
Combine milk and flavorings and put into mixture. Blend. Add balance of flour. Mix to smooth, don't over mix.
Fill cupcake cups half full.
Bake 375F for about 15 min. or done.
Cool before frosting

QUICK CREAM ICING

2 c. Conf. Sugar, Stick butter, Sm. Egg 5 Tbs. Hot Coffee or Water
Mix all above until smooth. Ice cupcakes. Use any desirable color or flavor as desired.

CHAPTER SEVENTEEN

Pouring rain with distant thunder made getting out of bed miserable. The false alarm at four o'clock am had pushed the envelope. The constant runs at all hours were beginning to render extreme anxiety.

"Sometimes I wish there'd be a real fire at that hotel," new firefighter Ellen exclaimed to Della. "Somebody is crazy!"

Della was closing the buttons on her uniform, "Middle of night is always rough. Solid sleep is so wonderful!"

"Tell me about it!" Ellen agreed. "It's weird when we run for nothing."

"One day that phathom character will slip up. Right now we do what we have to do," encouraged Della. They left the sleeping quarters for the kitchen.

Everyone was sipping coffee while reading their newspapers. The atmosphere was a bit bleak. Chief Thomas' footsteps echoed across the room. He placed a big box on the table. "Wake up everybody! Look what I brought! My wife got up early and made biscuits, gravy and stuff! I've got pull at my house!"

Todd responded, "Wow! We need it! We had another 4:00 am call!"

Chief, feeling irritated, remarked "Do I need to ask?"

"No! Another false alarm, same place just another time!" answered Gina Ballard. "Then we had another call during that one."

"Yes, those calls are more often and becoming worse. The second call was it legit?" Thomas asked.

"It was a trash can at the truck stop. Somebody threw a cigarette into it. Not much, but it could have turned out bad had a driver not found it when he did. Apparently, when he opened the door the bathroom was saturated with swells of smoke. We were nearby and could take the call. Only took us a few minutes to determine the first one was a false alarm."

"I see. These false alarms have to stop!" angrily contested the Chief. "Enough is Enough!"

They heard someone knock at the break room door. "Hey! I'm looking for Chief Thomas!"

It was the Police Chief Jayson Ball. Todd lifted his brow, "Come in, Chief is right here. Need coffee and breakfast?"

"Sounds great," he accepted. "I want to talk to each of you about these false alarms. Everyone says they are coming in more often."

The Police Chief had each firefighter to relate any information making his own notes. Breakfast was a turn for the better. Knowing the false alarms were being treated as a crime and seriously studied, appeased them, the fire crew, for the moment.

The phone rang shrilly. Ellen said, "Chief Thomas, you'd better take this!"

"Chief Thomas," the man answered. "Well, no, we didn't have anyone in that area checking for gas leaks. Give me your address and we'll be right there."

Thomas looked at Jayson Ball, "Come in here!" He motioned him to his office.

"I just had some people asking if we had anyone checking for a gas leak. First, That's not our job, the gas company attends to that. Second, our people aren't out there doing that. Sounds odd! The people who called were worried about something. How about riding with me to talk to them?"

"Be glad to, but I'll meet you there. I need my car with me. What's the address?" accepted Police Chief Ball.

They both left for 216 Seamore Drive about thirty blocks from the fire station. Chief Thomas arrived first. Immediately he bolted to the open door.

An elderly woman rushed to unlock the screen. "Thank you for coming! Please come in!"

"I'm glad you called. I'm Fire Chief Jerry Thomas. Someone else is on the way from the police department. What's your situation?"

"We had to let a firefighter in yesterday afternoon. He had a big pole stick and went around the house looking for a gas leak, at least he said."

"What is the name of the firefighter who came to your house?" Chief prompted. "Was he in one of our vehicles?"

"Yes, he was driving a car with the department name on it or I wouldn't have let him in," smiled the husband.

"His name?" continued Chief.

"I don't remember. It started with a, a, uh, with a 'c' I think," struggled the lady. "But I could recognize him. He was all by himself."

"Why did you wait to call now?" investigated the Fire Chief.

"We didn't know until it was time to take my medicine," offered the gentleman.

The Police Chief tapped at the door then entered, "Things alright?" he posed.

"Listen to this. Someone from the firehouse came yesterday and looked all over their place with some kind of pole stick pretending to be searching for a dangerous gas leak. We don't do that!" Fire Chief informed.

"I see," Chief Ball squinted his eyes. "We can check this out."

"They can identify him. Now they say their medicines are missing," added Fire Chief. "We'll easily trace this, I just can't imagine any one of our men doing such!" "Police Chief smiled. "How about we get pictures of fighter personnel and bring them here for you to identify this person. How old is he? Hair Color?"

The older woman replied, "He is about 45 or more. Hair is brown and a white man. He had a tattoo on his lower arm that was black and red. Couldn't see all of it though."

"I need to take my medicine," whined the man. "Nobody has been in our house but him for about a week."

"Maybe you misplaced it!" Chief Ball suggested.

"Hell No! I always put it in the bathroom cabinet. Come on, I'll show you!" He determined, "Everybody thinks if you're old you're crazy and can't remember! Humph!"

The bathroom was small so the Chief's took turns looking.

"Man I can't see any of our people doing such a thing," grieved Thomas. "I believe there's a problem at this house. Did you look around for your meds? Sometimes we start to do one thing and change in the middle then do something else."

"Hell no! I told you! Might figure you fellows are in cahoots with each other. We'd be up the creek is we needed the fire department for a real fire. We were just reporting the truth." Fussed the man. His wrinkled jaw twitched with anger.

"Just hear us out, we are concerned and will find out who is involved," consoled Chief Ball. "Our investigation is already started."

"What about our medicine? It's my blood pressure medicine I have to have it now!" teared the older guy. "This is real scary! You can't trust anybody!"

Fire Chief calmly touched his shoulder, "Tell me who your pharmacist is and I'll call for a temporary supply."

"That might help," blubbered the man, "But we don't have a way to get it."

"We'll pick them up for you!" Chief Thomas tried to restore the man's faith while making a few calls. "We'll be back soon. I definitely will check on all of this. Don't worry, things are alright."

The two city officials left the house and stood between their cars. Fire Chief sadly looked down trying to remember any recent odd situations. "This is so strange. Come on to the firehouse and let's get into our photographs."

Both cars returned to the station. The two men hustled into the chief's office.

"Do you remember anyone with a tattoo on his low arm?" quizzed the cop. "Everybody looks alike in these pictures."

"I know. Let's look for anyone about the age the couple revealed, I just can't understand this!" Thomas worried.

About a half hour passed as they studied the photos and possibilities. Finally, Chief Thomas declared, "I see three pictures you have selected. No, I can't believe this! Go ahead take them if you like. Maybe, just maybe it'll be something else. Could be someone outside the department!"

I'll get the medication and show them these face shots." Sighed the husky Police Chief. "It's hard to think our own could go off the grid! This is serious and especially if drug theft is involved. We just have to prepare ourselves."

"I know," replied Thomas with painful tears in his eyes. He thought of the photographs and parts of them raced through his mind. It would be the hardest thing he'd ever had to deal with, if one of his men had stooped to such. In fact, he wondered if he'd be able to continue being Fire Chief. The brotherhood of the department seemed at stake.

He felt his lips go numb, it seemed as if a horse was sitting on his chest. Then everything seemed to explode. Immediately he reached for a chair that slid out from under him. The floor was next. He fell motionless.

Chief Ball had left but Della heard the noise. She ran to Jerry Thomas and called out, "Get EMT – NOW!!"

Quickly someone responded. Help was nearby. Della urged everyone to step back while she took a fast look. Chief had a large cut on his head from the fall.

Immediately EMT entered. They released her, preparing Thomas for transport. The man was coming conscious enough to speak for himself. "I'm alright!" Chief Thomas pleaded. "Guess I tripped over that chair!"

"How do you feel now? We gave you oxygen when we got here." Informed the medic.

"Okay, just get me into a chair!"

"No, Chief you need to be checked. You're going to the hospital. You were blue around your mouth. We need you healthy!" Della pushed. "Take him in!"

Chief gave up as he remembered how he felt before the fall. At the emergency room, he was admitted into the hospital. It turned into a full afternoon event of test.

Della and Chief's wife were waiting for news. Finally, the doctor appeared. "He's going to be fine. Seems as if he had a bad fall. We are monitoring his heart too!"

"Oh God, he's had a heart attack!" whimpered the wife, June! She sat and put her hands over her face.

"No, he didn't have a heart attack! That's not what he said," scolded Della. "He's being checked out."

The doctor continued, "We're keeping him here. The fall gave him a concussion. We closed that cut on his head. He needs to be kept quiet."

"We'll do that, anything!" Jane whispered. "Can I stay with him?"

"Of course, we'll send a recliner chair so you can stay the night. When we have more news, I'll be back. He will come to his room soon." The man left quickly returning to the nurse's station. Obviously he was dispensing orders.

"I'll stay with you, Della said. "Thank you," she gratefully accepted. Jane was the second wife. They had been married for almost eighteen years. Her husband was a very handsome, gentle and caring man. He was totally supportive with all his family, church and crew. It made her feel proud to think of their wonderful life. She prayed to herself.

Della sat on a straight chair in the room that was designated for them. She tapped nervously on a small table, remembering earlier happenings of the day. "He left with the Police Chief to talk to some people about a gas leak. That was right at breakfast. We had another of those crank calls about a fire that was not. That's been going on for a long time."

"What are you saying," June inquired.

"Trying to think if he's been worried about something here!" Della replied. "Well, that's life. There's a new problem most every day."

Jane seemed stressed, "I hope the Police Chief has an idea of who has been making those false alarms."

"Maybe Commander Bailey? He has new issues all the time." whispered Della.

"We're all used to the Commander and his antics. I just believe something else upset him. This is different." Jane posed.

Della stepped into the hall to call the firehouse. Todd was anxiously waiting for news. "Hey girl, what's happening with the Chief?"

"Still not certain, we're waiting. There's something going on we don't know about. If you hear anything call me!" she cried. Her sniffing was loud.

"What do you mean?"

"Todd, the chief is still sort of out of it. He split his head when he fell. Look, they are running test on his heart; not good! Call the Police Chief and see what's going on; there's something."

Again, the doctor returned. At the same time Chief was brought to his bed. The personnel helped him slide from the mobile bed into his. "My rear is cold!" he shivered with eyes fixed on Jane.

"Hi, Baby," she smiled with optimism.

The doctor sat on the edge of the bed, "All test are in. We need to make plans."

"At worse, send me to Riverside Funeral Home!" joked Chief. "I'm fine."

"We're not there, but you have issues, very serious issues," began the doctor. "The EKG indicated some major concerns. We moved on to find just what was really happening. You did not have a heart attack but you do have major blockage in several arteries."

"Oh mercy!" mumbled the wife. "What should he do?"

"Do I need to have anything done right away. I really must get back to headquarters," prevailed the Chief.

"I suggest immediate surgery, like yesterday. You won't make it long like this. I've ordered a 24-hour supervision of a nurse until we can get you into surgery," continued the doctor. This is just luck that you didn't have a heart attack. We need to do bypass surgery. When we get in there we will know everything."

Jane felt weak in the knees but firmly held her husband's hand. "Of course! We want the best for him, don't we honey?"

"I've heard the food here is as good as the doctors! Bring it on!" he licked his dry lips, "Della, you get back to the station and get things in order. Have Captain to take over for me. This will be easy since Commander Bailey is on a ten-day leave. In Fact, perfect!"

All was put in order. Della left in shock to inform the fire crew and meet with Captain Williams.

The crew was at an open bay door pretending to oversee a truck. "Della, how's the Chief?" inquired Gina.

"Let's go in the break room," she ordered.

They reverently gathered around the long table while Della talked with Captain Williams. She felt he should have a report first. The urgency of it all seemed so grim but it was vital to step up and carry their weight. Everything had to be protected, city officials had to be notified and interim plans made.

Once Captain Williams took charge things reverted back to work as usual. He said, "Della, I want to talk to Chief Ball. We have to stop the false alarms! We don't have time to handle them."

Several days passed. John Ball parked into official parking and jolted into the firehouse, "Williams I need you!"

The two paired off into private space. They brought each up on all the current events and the Fire Chief's condition. His bypass surgery was unexpected but a success.

John conveyed, "I'll tell you, Chief is really worried. I have new news though. We were investigating a call at some older couple's house. I took pictures of department personnel to them. They said no one was the man that came to their house. I sent my sketch artist over and they described the person. I even had them to try to recall the tattoo the man had. They actually did a great job. We have someone being questioned. He's not a firefighter, he works in city garage. Looks like he would take a city vehicle off the maintenance lot and do his thing. He'd select certain people where he thought he could get prescriptions from. The fellas girlfriend worked at Craig's Drugs and gave him a list of people."

"Now that's policing! It will certainly take a tremendous worry off Chief Thomas. None of us could comprehend how it could be possible for one of us to do such!" Captain Williams sighed with relief. "What a horrendous thing to do! Have to say it's an original!"

"You're correct. We haven't arrested him yet though. It's vital to do a total investigation. There could be more people involved." Injected the cop. "Not a word to anyone, I mean nobody. Let's go to the hospital and check on Thomas. He will be relieved!"

"Come on! Let's make his day!" rationalized Williams.

"Don't forget, your Chief has been through major surgery. Would this be too much?"

"No! Oh no! I think it floored him when he thought a firefighter was involved!" Captain conveyed.

Soon the two happily slipped into the Chief's hospital room. He looked pale from his trauma. A nurse tried to stop them. "Wait outside!"

"No! I have to see them!" winced Thomas.

"God, this has been an ordeal having my chest sliced open! Look here! My zipper! This is my gift from God to always remind me how fortunate I am to be here!"

"You look good for the wear and tear!" smiled Captain Williams. "Man, I didn't know how much I loved you!"

Tears came to their eyes and they fought to not let go. When someone close goes to the edge it gauges the fear inside you. We all expect to die someday but we never think how close it could be.

"I'll be better than ever now. The toughest is behind me," he weakly said.

"That's so great. Are you ready for some good news?" asked Police Chief.

"Only good news from now on! Let me suck down my pills!" A nurse handed him a glass of water with pills in a cup. "Down the hatch!" she winked. He's the perfect patient! He has been such a good boy! Chief do you need anything?"

He shook his head no. "Can they stay just a little longer. They work with me!"

"Not much longer. You need rest!"

After she walked out, the two men walked closer smiling like the world was just beginning. They both blurted out, "We have the answer!"

"To what? I can't read your minds," whispered the Chief. "The calls, you settled it?"

The police official revealed, "Still working on that. The person doing the gas checking deal! We're 99% certain we have our man and a woman!"

His face saddened remembering the moments that lead up to his near "widow maker." Again, the stress appeared. He quietly grabbed his chest and pressed the call button. "Who is it?"

"Not a firefighter, Chief, this is nobody from your firehouse!"

Relief returned to the patient's soul. Color brightened his face, it all seemed like a new engine humming to perfection. When a nurse came in she inquired, "What can I do? Your monitor showed a change but leveled out."

"Guess I sat on some wires. I'm fine, perfect! Just better than ever! When can I get back to work?" Chief tried to justify the niche. "These men are my best friends! They will take care of anything!"

She smiled, "Talk to your doctor. Nurses do what they are told! Let me adjust your bed. By the way, did you urinate and have a B.M today?"

"Yep! On my on with a little help to that little room over there!" he grinned.

The whole "gas and meds" story was revealed quickly. The investigation would continue and become breaking news.

After a few more days in the hospital Fire Chief Thomas gathered his belongings to be dismissed. His wife Jane and a nurse rolled his hospital wheelchair to the front entrance.

"Aren't we going the wrong way?" Chief smiled, he pointed "The departing door is back there!"

"Oh? I didn't know that!" joked the nurse.

Down deep, the man thought it so strange that nobody came to help his wife take him home. He felt a bit empty not knowing exactly how after extensive heart surgery life would be. Everything seemed so quiet as they found the automatic doors.

But of course, there they were! Two big fire trucks, a cheering and happy crowd waving, whistling and shouting for him in this "Quiet Zone." Immediately a band from the local high school began playing. It felt so wonderful to be remembered and loved. Nothing could be finer for certain.

Chief stepped from his hospital chair and waved. Captain Williams, Della, Todd and Police Chief Ball rushed to him yelling pre-cautions but hugging, shaking hands while hundreds of red, white and blue balloons sailed upward.

They said together, "Good to get you back home, Chief!"

Someone rolled a red carpet from the door area of Engine 27. It stopped in front of the Chief. "Mac" gently walked down the bright path and stopped in front of him. The dog sat wagging his tail and let out two fast barks. A beautiful Dalmatian wearing a pink dress and seven little spotted puppies that looked just like "Mac" jumped from the truck hunkering down beside him. They sat staring at the Chief.

Everyone went wild with cheers watching the new family.

"Mac! What's this?" Thomas laughed. "Doing your part I guess!"

"Aren't they cute?" Della tried to defend the dog.

"Yes, they are beautiful. Just like all of this!" Tears swelled in his eyes. "Come on Jane, let's go home!"

She grabbed his arm and the crew helped them into the waiting fire engine with Mac and Molly and the puppies.

The short parade headed for the fire house a half mile away to enjoy a wonderful reunion.

Chief felt like his old self with a "zipper" in his chest. He knew now he was ready to tackle his job better than ever. His whole firehouse and fire department was greatly his making. They had shared the best in their lives and as well, the worst. Each firefighter was so individual with special needs and private ventures. It totaled to a life worthwhile.

PUMPKIN SPICE BISCOTTI

Set oven to 350 degrees
1 cup chopped walnuts (add a little flour, shake and set aside.)
¼ lb. butter (stick)
2 Jumbo Eggs
1 cup Pumpkin (Libby's can)
½ cup granulated Sugar and
½ cup Brown Sugar (dark)
2 cups Plain Flour
¾ cup Self-rising Flour
1 Tbs. Baking Powder
Dash Salt
½ tsp. Almond Extract &
½ tsp. Vanilla Flavoring
1 ½ Tbs. Pumpkin Spice (powdered)

1. Mix wet ingredients until smooth (Mixer)

2. Place all dry ingredients in bowl. Add to wet mixture until blended. Fold in nuts.

3. Roll onto floured surface and make three long rolls. Place on cookie sheet lined with parchment paper leaving at least three inches apart. (should be 8" long). Place in oven for 30 to 40 minutes until light brown. TURN OVEN DOWN TO 300 DEGREE.

4. Cool for 6 minutes then cut on diagonal with sharp knife. Return to Cookie sheet with parchment paper and bake another 8 to 10 minutes. Turn each cookie over and back an additional 8 minutes.

5. Remove to cooling rack. Let cool and dry then store and enjoy.

CHILI

(2 to 3 Servings)

1/3 lb. Turkey (no fat) ground

1 tsp. Olive Oil

Chop and Stir til near done in fry pan

(Sprinkle with salt substitute)

Add ¼ cup chopped Onion

¼ cup chopped Green Pepper

3 small Tomatoes chopped

Stir in and simmer 10 minutes

1 cup Pintos & Broth (home cooked)

Add: 1 Tbs. Chili Powder (or to taste)

½ tsp. Garlic Powder

½ tsp. Cajun Spice

1 cup Ketchup

1 cup Water

Simmer at least ½ hour

Cover and Serve

CAKE IN MUG

Cake –
4 Tbs. Flour
3 Tbs. Sugar
2 Tbs. Cocoa (or Chocolate Syrup)
1 Egg
3 Tbs. Milk
3 Tbs. Oil or Butter
½ tsp. Vanilla
1 Tbs. Chips (chocolate)
Take Dry mixtures – mix well
Add Eggs (beaten) and mix
Add Oil, Milk – Mix
Stir in Chips
Place in 2 Mugs
Microwave 3-5 minutes
Serve

CARMEL POUND CAKE RECIPE

All ingredients at room temperature, but eggs. Blend
3 Sticks Butter
½ tsp. Salt
3 cups Sugar
7 Large Eggs – add in and check each Egg as you add them. Blend until they disappear.
Ready: Pan Pound Cake or Angel Food Pan – Make collar atop with wax paper Dust with plain Flour

Add:
2 ¾ cup Plain Flour
½ Tbs. Baking Powder
¼ cup Self-Rising Flour
Add flavoring (at ½ point of flour)

1 tsp. Vanilla Flavoring
2 Tbs. Almond
Cook at 320 for 1 hour 23 minutes

Mix

1 cup Butter
½ cup Cocoa
2 cups Flour
2 cups Sugar
4 Eggs
4 tsp. Vanilla Flavoring1 cup Chopped Nuts
3 x 13 Pan
Bake 20-25 minutes

CHAPTER EIGHTEEN

The overwhelming scream of the buzzers and persistent clanging from the bells blasted once more, 4:10 am blinked on all the digital clocks. Again duty personnel snapped to their positions meeting this early morning call. Everyone was silent until the first directions penetrated the system.

It seemed they all groaned together "Oh No!"

Shortly the huge Engine 28 was in motion engaging the street with force. Della observed, "Back to the old hotel again. This could be the bad one!"

Sounding nearly hopeful Todd agreed. "At this time of day it could be for real."

With no traffic, they arrived in minimal time.

"Look!" Della spotted. "There's big smoke out back!"

"Those windows are squeezing out smoke too!" added Todd. He tightened his helmet and joined the crew around Capt. Williams. Observing the situation at hand his instant plan was revealed and the firefighters proceeded into their role for the fight. Equipment was moved into place and dispatch was already sending more truck and assists.

The place now looked bright as high noon. The fire was gaining force as it lapped through the tired old worn out hotel that should have been condemned. The forty some rooms of the 3 story building was full of old dirty debris, dust and grime.

Quickly they dispersed duty hauling equipment from their truck. Williams was calling orders. They opened the doors, several firefighters rushed into the rickety old building.

There was a loud screech, then a boom! Five firefighters felt the movement as the bottom dropped from beneath their feet. It was shocking to feel the fast tumble downward to what seemed like another world. Thick smoke engulfed the whole basement. They forced themselves to gain composure finding new positions.

"Grab onto this line! I brought it with me!" yelled one firefighter. "Come on!"

Immediately they could see the blaze ahead of them through scattered debris of saved trash."

"It's serious, My God!" screamed Gina Ballard as she clung to the endless line. "We could be trapped down here!"

They heard a man moaning, "I can't move!"

Burney Easter, a new hire from a nearby city called out, "Hold on man! I'm coming!"

As Burney reached the downed firefighter, the others continued to battle the blaze and called to Captain Williams their status.

Above them, the rest of the crew was fighting the wild blaze from overhead and seemingly everywhere. It was devastating trying to pull the crew wherever needed.

"Carl! Call headquarters from the truck. Tell them to order everyone available here. Get the Fire Chief too!" Williams rushed. "It's out of control already and our people are struggling! Go!"

Fireman Carl Blair, another new hire, was amazed but pressed on to carry out instructions. As he finished the contact with headquarters, a yellow fire truck rebound to a stop and a ladder truck from another community department joined them. At the same time their snorkel truck pulled in.

With the correlation of orders, Williams was gaining slight control. "We must search inside this nasty old hotel! Be sure we get all the people out now!"

Blue streams of light seemed to be frozen in mid-air above. Flames deliberately ate their way through the attic as the rolling smoke escaped from the continual water being poured everywhere. You could hear deep growling, sapping, thudding and people screaming. "Help!" yelled a woman in a robe calling from a window. "Help me!"

Williams demanded, "Get her! That's the woman in charge! She can't find her way! Throw the snorkel to that window!"

Immediately, she was snatched from the opening and brought to safety.

All emergency equipment joined into the battle. An ambulance rushed away with several building tenants needing attention. They were all coughing, chocking and trying to get their breath. They were terrorized of the situation.

The old woman was crying in desperation, "What happened? I ain't done nutting wrong! Oh, dang it! I hurt everywhere!"

Captain tried to console her, "Go to the hospital, they'll help. We will get this under control! You'll be fine!"

An EMT coaxed her, "Come on lady!" He more or less dragged her into a waiting unit. Quickly it flashed its way into the darkness.

Ladders were to the edge of the hotel entryway where the floor had fallen in from the weight of the responders and equipment. Another crew hustled to the edge to rescue and guide the endangered crew below.

"Come on!" roared visiting Chief Pete Masters, beaconing with his light, "This way out! Come on! Williams sent me for you."

The five were gagging, coughing and wheezing as they urgently battled to follow the rescue light and route to a ladder. They struggled in their heavy gear to ascend the step-rounds. The rescue crew powerfully threw in more line and talked them to safety away from the lapping flames and horrid smoke.

Once topping the exit out, each firefighter rolled to the ground removing broken torn protective clothing. A stream of water was forced their way to be positive that no fire was in their turn out gear.

"Oh God! I didn't expect that!" cried Gina. We've been in that building before!"

"Old buildings can be any kind of hazard!" Chief Pete informed. "They have all kind of hidden waiting disasters. We got you just in time. This building is full of structure failures from decay, rot, bad material and re-dos along with pest and critters. This burned enough that the floors fell beneath you!"

"Oh, God!" I'm sick!" moaned Gina as she threw up. Several exclaimed they saw their life pass before them. Spewing violent red and blue streaks of flames forced everyone to move back from the charring mass as it mixed spewing greater destruction, a very terrible and dangerous event.

Captain Williams directed crews to encompass the area with a bigger safety zone. On-lookers never consider their own risk for safety nor the needs of the fire crews. People often follow fire trucks for the excitement of trauma.

Orders continued to try to banish the huge fire kindled from the over one-hundred-year structure. Their massive efforts working for the cause were bringing the huge fire finally within control. The building and its outbuildings covered a half block. All calls would now stop as with routine of these fires.

This would be the end of all the fake calls to this old hotel. It should have been condemned years before yet somehow never was forced to update.

Time crafted the place as a total disaster with the yellow caution – 'Don't enter tape.' People still drove past to view the remains. The crews finally returned to the firehouse. Everyone was worn hungry and exhausted.

People aren't aware of what we faced!" Della acknowledged. "We could have all been slaughtered!"

"Yeah!" shivered Gina. "I thought I was going to die! It was unreal, awful!"

"This is what we do!" reminded Captain walking past them. "We are proud of everybody! Thank God, we're all safe and that chapter is about closed!"

"Really? Closed? Looks like somebody should investigate the thing! It was beyond routine! Look at the hundred times we were sent there!" growled Della. "I would like to see the face of that property owner!"

"That's right! Who owned the old ragged shack!" Gina injected. "The scum bag didn't care about anything!"

"We are definitely proceeding to contact him and instill what it will take to recover the cities loss..."

"But, Captain" Della teared up. "How do you repay our emotional trauma as well as the physical? Look at my arm!"

"Girls! I can't tell you how amazed and proud I am that you are on my crew. Yeah, we have to rush to the end! Keep in mind, it's a passion that we sign up for. When the bells ring that's our signal to fly. We all do it! A firefighter has to be selfless, underpaid, above the ridicule and dedicated to the purpose. You know how it is! It is what it is!" sighed Captain.

The two women smiled as they mentally relived the moments of what it takes, the getting there and back.

"We know," Della encountered. "In spite of it all, it's vital we understand. Look at all the calls to the old hotel we made. That wasn't easy. Two o'clock, three o'clock until six o'clock in the morning never came easy."

"Come to think about it, we might start missing those early trips!" laughed Gina. "Think about the good food everybody sent us!"

They looked at each other as they shuffled to pull out chairs. Another crew had rushed in to replace them in the event of another fire. They too found places at the table.

"Look at that chicken!" smiled Todd. "Here Della, get the first piece!"

She saw a gleam in his eyes. He winked as he forked a beautiful chicken breast on a plate and placed it before her. Their eyes met and fingers touched when he added the biscuit. They both giggled sitting side by side. Their "secret" was about to pop seams. Nobody had chanced romance at the work ever before. Might have been an unwritten law.

Captain laughed, "Everybody eat up! We have to get rest now. We will have a meeting tomorrow. All of the film and paperwork will be complete by then!"

It didn't take long for the exhausted crew to begin leaving for their homes. Della and Todd left in her van.

"Where to?" the man lifted his brows. "I have something you need to see."

"My house!" she whispered.

"I'll try not to speed!" he teased.

Once they were inside, the two clung to each other. Tears bubbled up in Della's eyes. She whispered, "I love you!"

"I love you too! You are everything to me." Todd confirmed.

Quickly, he dropped to a knee and reached for her hand." Sweetheart, will you marry me?"

She looked up and watched him flash a beautiful diamond. "Oh Todd! Todd! Oh yes! Yes!"

He slipped the ring on her left hand ring finger and they gently kissed, cried and exclaimed their love.

Soon they sat together on the sofa continuing to celebrate with excitement.

"We have been through so very much. In all this time I have felt your love in every aspect of my life," stated Della.

"I know, me too!" He paused. "Nothing matters anymore – except I Love you and want to be together forever. Whatever it takes, If I have to quit the job, so be it!"

"You wouldn't be happy doing that. I can be the one to change jobs. Might be fun to just be a wife!"

Todd lit up. "How about a baby one day?"

"Oh yes! Little "Toddy." She gleed.

"We can cross that when it comes. Big question is now we are engaged – When do we get married?" smiled the tall handsome man.

"Maybe in a couple of years?" teased Della.

"Humph!" he grunted sadly. "Years? They do that to get married? Gosh, dang we can't be that long!"

"You're right, how about two days?" Della conceded.

"Now you're talking! Two days! Great! Great! Terrific!" Todd stood quickly. "How? Where? When? Women know this stuff!"

"We'll get dressed up, find a preacher and slip it by the Captain!" Della nearly screamed with joy. "We have our house here, you move in. The lawyer can change the title in five minutes. We can do it best to have a simple affair. Captain Williams and Gina can stand up for us. They'll do it!"

"A perfect plan! Let's call them now! They need to come over! I brought a bottle of champagne!" Todd almost yelled.

"Now? They'll kill us!"

"Maybe its quick but they'll have to deal with it! Call Gina, I'll call Captain," he moistened his lips then kissed his fiancé.

They both snapped up their cell phones to put the plan into action. Neither would take no for an answer. So, whatever tale they chose was good enough.

After they placed their phones on a table they looked at each other and yelled:

"She's coming!"

"He's coming!"

"When?" Della giggled.

"Now!" Todd shivered. "Now!"

They went into each other's arms and danced around and around.

"You answer the door and I'll straighten up!"

"Alright, let me get the bottle I hid in your wheels."

Within twenty minutes a knock banged on the door. Both Gina and Captain stood on the porch then proceeded to enter. They could see the couple locked together.

"What's this mouth to mouth resuscitation? Supposed to be laying down for that!" Captain teased.

They twisted around, proudly extending Della's hand to show off the engagement ring. Both were on cloud 999!

"My God!" Gina exclaimed. "When?"

"A bit ago, isn't it beautiful?" Della blushed happily.

"You two deserve happiness. No more sneaking, hiding and tale talking. Good for you!" Captain exclaimed. "When is the big day?"

"Day after tomorrow!" the couple replied together.

"Two days?" squeaked Gina. "How can you do it?"

"That's why we called you two! We need advice and help," smiled the bride to be looking proudly at her hand then to the groom.

"We want to help but two days is impossible!" advised the Captain.

Della felt the blood drain from her face at the thought. "Why? We have waited already; it's been so long."

Captain grinned, "You need at least three days. We need to do this on a Saturday. Three days will be a Saturday."

The couple lit up. Their fears of being caught had returned but again vanished. "Oh, you devil!" Della giggled. "Nothing is standing in our way!"

"Fine, how about Saturday at 2:00 pm at the firehouse?" Todd quizzed. "Can you clear that for us? We'll see if the Chief can officiate. You know he has his license to do that."

"Whatever makes you two happy!" the boss suggested.

Todd flipped the cork from the champagne. Glasses were raised for toast by the four friends.

Gina asked, "What about both of you being at the department. Getting married might be a problem."

"Who cares?" Todd acknowledged. "We'll cross that bridge when it comes. Right now, I'm living on love!"

They spent a few hours planning and reaching towards the future.

CREAMED CORN

8 to 12 Fresh Corn (on Cob)
Shuck (Remove Husks)
Water
½ tsp. Salt
¼ tsp. Sugar
½ Stick Butter
Plain Flour (2 Tbs. more or less)
1 Can Evaporated Milk
½ cup water as needed

Place cut corn in large frying pan, add salt, sugar and butter. Bring to full boil and stir constantly. Don't let stick. When corn changes color (lighter) carefully sprinkle in flour (don't let it get lumpy). Then, add milk slowly and thin with water as necessary. Keep loosely stirring until right thickness. If you get too thin sprinkle in a little more flour, or cornstarch, if too thick add water as needed.

SLICED SWEET POTATO PIE

1 Homemade Pie crust
3 Med. Sweet Potatoes, cooked and sliced
1 cup Milk (Canned Milk)
1 tsp. Vanilla

Sugar Mixture:
1 Stick Butter at room temperature
1 cup Sugar
1 cup Light Brown Sugar
1 tsp. Cinnamon and 1 tsp. Nutmeg

Grease a deep-dish pan and line with your favorite pie crust. Fill with one layer of sliced cooked sweet potatoes. Cream together butter, sugar, brown sugar, cinnamon, nutmeg. Spread over sweet potato slices. Repeat potato layers and sugar mixture until pan is almost filled. Combine milk and vanilla, pour over filling. Cover with top crust if you like.

Bake 1 hour at 325 degrees.

SALMON STEW

2 lbs. Salmon (clean, skin, no bones)
Slice Thin – Salt to Taste
½ Stick Butter
1 Very Small Chopped Onion
2 Tbs. Chopped Parsley (fresh if possible)
1 Tbs. Coarse Pepper
1 ½ Cans Evaporated Milk
1 ½ Cups Water
¼ Cup Ketchup (Warm)
2 Cups 2% Milk
Ready all items for Stew -
Place butter in large stew pot
Add: Salmon, Onion, Parsley, Salt, Pepper
Sauté: for about 8-10 minutes, stir slightly
Add: Evaporated Milk and Water bring to near boil
Add: 2% Milk and Ketchup, stir in lowly.

CHAPTER NINETEEN

The fire house was packed with involved firefighters and personnel. Everyone was quiet with anticipation waiting for Chief Thomas. They were anxious to hear the statistics on the hotel and move on. No one could guess the outcome. Constant calls and now nothing!

Three days had passed since the devastating ordeal of the old flop house. Somehow, when you drove by the ruins, it felt very sad. The many years of its past represented an amazing part of the history of the city and area. Presidents, Governors, beauty queens, movie stars, Elvis as well as many ordinary people had graced that building. Aggravating as the calls were, now they seemed like nothing.

The Chief walked to the head of the table as if it were another day. He was dressed in his "formal" uniform. The others looked around at each other and smiled.

"Don't he look sharp!" exclaimed one man.

"Yeah!" agreed others.

"Let me have your attention, please!" Chief Thomas began.

The room became so quiet you could hear people breathing.

He continued, "We extended this meeting until now. It took more time to have all results of the hotel fire complete. This has been such a problem racing to the late night calls and the drama. How many of you have driven past that place in these last days after?"

There was almost a total show of hands. Each looked sadly around.

"The fire was a complete destruction. No way it can be renovated, not any part or out building. Even so, the place was already to be condemned. A shame that along with many of our historic buildings, it has to disappear. But for clean-up, it's gone."

"Chief, who owns the place?" called out a firefighter. "I'll get to that. Give me a minute," the man replied. "In spite of all the stress we've experienced, there is a dual outcome. We know who made the alarm calls and who the owner is."

You could hear the groans, moans and whispers. Chief let it quickly sink in as the people exchanged shocked words.

"Captain Williams, bring the people in from my office." He motioned with a twist of his head, clearing his throat. "Very shortly you will meet the culprits who made the false alarms. It's really a tragic fact that this was something fun to do!"

The door opened. Three young boys about 12 to 13 years old entered with the Captain. All three were clean cut, well dressed with tears rolling down their cheeks. Everyone could hear them blubbering.

Chief Thomas motioned them to stand next to him. As they stood being observed by the fire personnel he said nothing. The boys continued weeping and wiping their eyes. Everyone starred with open mouths.

Chief shook his head, "Here are the people who called us out time after time during those nights. We checked our records, they made about 128 calls. This proves that you never get by forever. Their parents are here with them and agree they should face the department. We will have conclusive findings with the City Attorneys. This is a very serious crime.

Williams stepped up, "They will be indicted as minors. As hard as it's been, it is a past situation. These kids were wanting to watch our trucks run for excitement. Believe me, they will know the full meaning of a criminal act. They did turn themselves in once the old hotel burned. That was not their doing. It put fear into them. When it burned, they were home. Guilt forced them to thinking they would be accused of setting fire to the hotel which would be horrible."

"That's right!" They came to us the next day to confess," Chief acknowledged. "Let them go back to my office."

People wanted more answers. Still Chief Thomas continued, "We found the hotel was burned due to several bucket of paint, thinner, turpentine and clean-up rags. Apparently a wire from a drop cord ignited with the chemicals. It could have happened at any time. Negligence! Pure neglect! We're all fortunate no one was killed. We are more fortunate that our fire crew rushed when the call came in."

Della raised her hand, "Who's the property owner?"

"Commander Bailey," replied their boss. "Our Commander Bailey. He of all people should at the very least kept the property up to code!"

"Commander Bailey?" screamed a dozen firefighters and crew members, "Commander Bailey?! Really?"

"No! It can't be!" Todd objected. "Even the Commander is smarter than to have a filthy crazy place like that!"

"It was just an investment for him!" insisted Captain Williams. "There's no law that says he can't buy a piece of property."

"Law says you have to maintain though." Della projected! "There is so much he could have done knowing we were getting all the calls and how hard it was on us."

"Right! We took a lot of abusive insults and punishment from Commander in these past years," Todd reminded them. "I nearly quit my job a few times because of him!"

"That Jackass!" screamed Gina. "He hated women being here unless you were cleaning or cooking." Ass said, 'A woman's place is in the home', as if we were servants. He deserves to be kicked you know where by each of us!"

Captain Williams could see the contempt in the eyes of everyone. Tears rolled down many of their cheeks. They relived the hurt and humiliation shared from the continual episodes that had factored. Captain needed to restore a positive reconstruction of their well-being.

"Let's all bow our heads and thank God for each other and be grateful for the plight we are now serving. Take each other's hand and remember the oath we live by. Let God give us strength to go on. We will have a moment of silence." Williams waited some minutes and smiled. "Thank you!"

The phone rang to interrupt the quiet. Chief Thomas quickly rushed from the room to answer it.

Immediately the group was buzzing about these current events. Much was said to get the shock of the "owner" and Commanders ownership into perspective.

After several minutes Chief Thomas returned. He tapped with a knife on an empty cup to gain order.

"Folks, I have some news for you. He began, regardless of what we think now and our disappointments in these last days. This will still be tough. The call was about Commander Bailey."

"Huh? Bailey?" murmured Gina. "Can't be good!"

"No it isn't!" Chief began. "Remember he left on a fishing trip for his vacation?"

Most people gestured yes.

"Well," Thomas was searching for words, with a dry mouth, "He had a heart attack!"

"Is he alright?" squired Della. "Well, No! Apparently he fell off his boat in deep water. They couldn't get help to save him. He either drowned or died immediately from the heart attack."

"Oh! Wow!' Gina sighed, "Ain't that something else!"

"Let's take a break now," Chief concluded. "We'll get back here in two hours. I will discover more from the family and pass it on to you as we learn more."

"What happened, happened!" Todd pointed out as the phone rang again.

Chief answered again and stepped outside.

Looking at each other the fire crews and friends began to chat with concern.

Once more Thomas returned holding his hands into fists over his head. "That was Commander Bailey's son. He wanted us to know Bailey's remains will be sent home in several days after their investigation there at Virginia Beach, just to confirm there was no foul play. He won't have a regular funeral but later there will be a simple service. We will be informed."

Captain Williams replied, "That will be good. We'll pass on that info when it comes."

"By the way," Chief Thomas smiled, "On the wonderful side of life. We are all invited to be here at 4:00. Had to change the time from 2:00. It's a special event. Don't be late!"

"A party?" screeched a firefighter. "Yes! Be there. Dress up! We'll celebrate!" the Chief suggested. "That's only a few hours."

Todd reasoned with logic, "Look forward to later! At least old buddy Commander Bailey won't be there to soil this!" He thought back to many miserable situations with him.

"You're Right!" Della injected.

"How about this! The old boy fished his life away! Guess he did leave this world doing what he really loved," another firefighter inserted.

"Yeah!" Gina grinned mischievously. "It's funny how Bailey always talked about his last ride to be in that big silver Cadillac hearse that we see at the funeral home."

Todd looked down then laughed. "The world has changed so much. Funeral stuff is not the same. The old day people sat around all night for days with the dead person, now most everybody is cremated."

"True," laughed Gina. "Guess they plan to burn his ass to send him home!"

Todd stated, "Probably! See! Then the big silver Cadillac is now replaced with something else, probably a little red Mini Van!"

"What an exchange! Cut your wings broken feathers!" stumbled Gina. "He Needs to be………."

"It's all in life!" Della felt tears. "It's life, time, then you die! We need to make the best of what we have!"

Todd remembered, "Hey! We have a party at 4:00. We have to get ready."

"Come on!" smiled Della grabbing Todd's hand.

BIG BIRTHDAY SHEET CAKE

2 ½ sticks butter

2 ¾ cups sugar

3 Tbs. very hot water

6 eggs (separated)

3 cups White Lilly plain flour or Soft as Silk Cake Flour

¾ cup White Lilly self-rising flour

3 Tbs. baking powder

½ cup sour cream

1 ½ cup evaporated milk

½ cup water

Mix creamed butter and sugar 8 minutes at low speed.

Add hot water – mix 2 more minutes

Let sit for 5 minutes.

Add egg yolks

*Have all dry ingredients ready

*Place all wet ingredients ready

Cream in alternately dry and wet items

Fold in stiffly beaten egg whites

Pour into ready sheet pan (12x16x2)

Bake 345 degrees for about 40 minutes.

(Dump on powdered wax paper and ice when cold.)

ICING

2 ½ cups confectioners' sugar

1 ½ cups soft butter

1 egg

1 cup Hershey Chips

(If you want white icing leave out chocolate chip and ad more confectioners' sugar if needed.)

1 tbs. Crisco

¼ cup powder cocoa

Blend all with hand blender to spread consistency. If thick add drops of water until you desired solution. Remember icing will thicken as cooled.

CHAPTER TWENTY

A most weather perfect day in May was smiling its happy treat. The morning had been filled with meetings of trauma and information. All the earlier transitions had been settled and tucked away. The fire station had emptied of all people other than the current staff.

"Time is passing fast!" observed Captain. "The weather is ready, so how about the rest of the plans?"

"We're on it!" acknowledged a firefighter within sound. "Believe me, Gina has everyone in the park right across the street. Look, they are working like mad!"

The front door opened to view the full sight of the Memorial Park. Many amazing parties, reunions, important events and weddings had been staged there. Now, the whole Fire Department was involved in the most important item of all. The soon to be wedding for Della and Todd was on everyone's schedule of plans and great wishes.

Looking passed the open door, you could see white, pastel pink and blue balloons softly floating within the trees and shrubs. The slight breeze was made to order. There must have been fifty firemen and spouses pulling the plan together.

A group of young girls in shorts were squealing like babies anxiously placing an extremely long 4' wide white aisle runner from the entry to the speaker stand. They were having to stabilize the item to be certain nobody tripped or that it would fly away.

More balloons with ties were knotted to cling at various places. Fire fighter Jones exclaimed, "How do you like this?"

They quickly stretched yards and yards of crepe-paper stringers throughout the entry way bushes and a super bigness evolved.

"How did you find that?" laughed Gina who had taken charge.

"Was easy, the clerk said to do it! Della will be happy! Jones grinned adding a big star to the front of the stage.

"Wait a minute! Dunce!" ranted Gina interrupting the plan. "A Big Star? Fool this is a wedding not Christmas!"

"Alright, I'll move it! It just looked so glorious!" he replied.

"You are gaudy!" Gina added. "Get rid of it!"

"Have it your way. Todd and Della are the stars!" he mumbled as he removed it.

"Tell you what, place it out by the street as a marker for the wedding place!" Gina retracted. "Perfect idea there!"

Grabbing the star, he attached it at an obvious spot before the entrance.

Things were focused into place. I's dotted and t's were crossed! All the effort rushed to an exquisite gala look that shouted wedding everywhere. The excess crew stood back to admire their handiwork.

"Perfect! Perfect! Perfect!" cried Gina joyfully. "I've got to go! Della is home waiting for me!"

Immediately, a group of catering trucks drove to the assigned tables to set up the lavish meal for the who knows how many people. This was a group financed party by all the fire personnel and families. Had to be exactly right.

As they began assembling their silver and crystal onto the food tables several relatives of the fire fighters arrived carrying huge pots.

"This is heavy!" exclaimed a very old lady. "This is Todd's favorite, chicken and dumplings!"

"Really?" smirked another elderly mom. "I have something even better! Just picked it up from the BBQ House!"

"Humph! What is it?" first granny asked.

"Ain't saying" the gran-lady giggled. "Todd totally loves this!"

"What?!"

"If you insist! Six BBQ possums! Look at them! They are perfect!" she gloated. "My great nephew went night hunting three nights ago. Did good didn't he!"

The two compared Todd's secret delicacies.

"Recon this woman he's hooking up with will understand the way he eats?" the BBQ granny wondered.

"Yeah, she'll eat the same things! She's tough, a fire fighting girl!"

The two women gave their contributions to the caterer who included both dished into the menu.

"They laughed while sneaking away. "Bet there won't be any left over. Todd ain't going to like those tiny little sandwiches. Did you see that?" giggled a granny. "They ain't big enough for a mouse!"

Most everyone was leaving the decorated park with total satisfaction. They each glanced approvingly over their shoulder to remember the elaborate scene.

An old bakery truck rattled across from the food tents and stopped. Immediately they went to work the catering tables designated for them. The white lace table cloths glistened in the sun. The florist had delivered all the magic that could be found in the sweet smelling bouquets and arrangements. All was put into place. From the station house, everything seemed perfect. It looked good, smelled good, and was fantastic. It was now pushing 4:00 pm.

Guests began to arrive. Some in department uniforms, turn-out gear and formal attire for men. Women jumped straight from the fashion magazine pages. They wore long and short; soft, sexy, elegant as well as plain plus the when necessary uniform.

"Look at that!" pointed the Chief. "I am not certain we will ever recover. The world is here! The governor, mayor and all the la-de-da's around town! This city certainly has a big mixture of folks.

"How wild!" replied Todd. "Sure am glad I have a front seat!"

"I knew if we'd walk from here it would be best," Chief looked into a mirror to adjust his tie. "I believe we should have done this in a grocery store. We may not have enough food!"

"Somebody start praying that Jesus will turn the loaves and fishes into enough for this multitude!" cracked the Captain. "Don't worry it will be alright!"

"Yeah! One pickle, one cracker and two sips of punch!" grieved the wedding host. "Where did all these additional people come from? Hundreds! Oh my gracious!"

A man knocked at a bay door and entered quickly, "Chief, we have sent our trucks back to the cater house to get every bit of the food we can find. We have lots frozen and it will be ready once we start serving."

Chief brightened as he shook hands with Bob Miller owner of Miller Catering and Baking. "Oh, God sent you to cut up the bread and fishes!"

"Not really, but I had a hunch that a crowd would gather! Don't worry we'll take care of them. The only thing is we don't have but one fire truck wedding cake! We have cookies and cupcakes for the rest!"

"This is a unique and weird affair!" entered Captain. "You guys about ready to cross the street and take our places?"

"Almost!" Chief smiled. He looked so elegant in his formal dress fireman uniform that sported all of the badges of honor he had acquired through the job.

"Thank you Bob for having our back!"

"Nothing to it! This is well deserved! It's wonderful!" exclaimed Bob Miller.

They shook hands.

Chief grinned quickly, "I've got a secret!"

"What?" quizzed those in the room.

"We can't let this out until next week but I did feel Todd should know before his honeymoon next week, we'll do a thing later."

"Know what?" Todd stared at the Chief.

With a smile and tear, the man said, "Todd, you are going to replace old Commander Bailey. 100% vote and you're legitimately in line for the position."

The group screamed "congratulations!" and slammed Todd's back until his jacket nearly dropped off.

"Oh Lordy! Thank you! Thank you!" Todd cried with real tears, "I was afraid I wouldn't be able to afford my wife!"

"You'll get there!" Bob consoled.

A voice over the fire house speaker interrupted, "Alright guys! Stop trying to get away! Everybody is waiting for the groom!"

Opening the door, they could hear music from across the street in the park. At a closer pace; the three, Groom Todd, Chief Thomas and Captain Williams, found the white satin walkway between the mass of friends and folks. They happily and slowly followed the chords of the string band of violins, harp and xylophone. People were everywhere. Emotions were high with the perfect plan of elegance that overwhelmed the spirit.

They eased into place on the stage area, the Chief stood in the middle, Todd to his left and his best man Captain Williams to the right. The crowd started to chuckle gently. Mac, the fire dog, walked down the aisle cloth and took his place beside Todd, as if anticipated. The men looked at each other and raised eyebrows in approval. Now the four watched the end of the aisle in expectation.

Once more the procedure continued with a beautiful love song of promise that many had melted hearts before "Oh Promise Me". As this message from the Gods was finished, the string band started the wedding march.

A white limousine pulled up in front of the Park entry. The driver quickly moved around the vehicle to open the back passenger doors. Gina, who was the Maid of Honor, slipped out first wearing a long, tiny, sleeveless Red dress that split to the knees on each side. Her blonde hair was shining like pure gold as she shook her head gently to distribute it to settle into place.

The limo driver held his gloved fingers toward the inside of the huge long vehicle; slowly a feminine hand reached for him. All eyes were glued for the appearance of the passenger. Gently, with easy movements a beautiful woman slipped from the seating. Once at the walkway, Gina fussed around her to situate all the beautiful ecstasy of her wedding gown into exact place and slipped the 25-foot veil softly to flow behind. This was the bride, Della, looking her most sophisticated and elegant best, not in turn out gear!

The crowd gasped with approval. Everyone was smiling.

The limo driver removed his hat and extended his arm for Della to join him at the aisle. Limousine driver was her father. Her mother accompanied them by taking Gina's hand to proceed down the white path.

"Daddy! I've waited so long!" whispered the bride to her father.

"I know, baby!" You now have everything!" he cuddled her to his side as the "Wedding March" called them.

The two paced down the path to meet the groom.

Once at the front, the father handed his daughter to her husband to be. He stepped aside to couple with his wife.

Della's gown was of white French lace over satin. It snuggly enhanced her usually hidden figure. The three quarter sleeves and open neck gave way to simplicity. A slight train made way for movement. The jeweled crown clung to the extreme trailing of silk opaque net and lace. In the late afternoon blissful sky, the low sun painted sparkling white diamond effects over the elegant stones hand sewn over the gown.

"That dress! Where did you find such a perfect fit?" cried Gina as tears dropped from her eyes. She witnessed a new woman that she had never known. Della the firefighter always in charge and wearing men's designed uniforms had turned into a soft charming beauty. "I hope one day I'll be able to find my someone."

Della winked as she heard the dream. "I've had my dress for four years! It's been in my closet all along!"

"Oh! Four years!" whispered and pointed Gina. "Oh, God! Look at that!"

At the beginning of the white satin path stood a beautiful Dalmatian who was snow white with many black spots. She had a ribbon bow around her head with a petite tiara and a bit of white mesh trailing behind her.

Della smiled, "It's alright Molly! Come!"

Gently the famous creature slowly walked to the bride. She sniffed at Mac and smiled widely. The two Dalmatians stood together waiting.

All eyes were now finally on Chief Thomas who was trying to contain himself. The animal couple presented another wrinkle in what had been a smooth start. The light whine of instruments brought a sweet touch.

"Friends, I want to welcome you to our congregation gathered to support the fire department and our two couples pledging their love for each other," he started. "A perfect time for us all is when we gather in love, faith and commitment. You have entrusted the whole city for us. Now, we want to thank you for this allegiance and sharing this special day to recover from old alliances and spin in the new."

The applause was nearly like thunder. People looked side to side appreciating their neighbor.

The Chief continued, "It is my greatest pleasure to be an ongoing part of such a wonderful event. Now, Della and Todd if you will join me here. This place has extended the love and happiness to many before you. We invite you all to accept the meaning of their love to be with them forever.

The couple held hands and pledged their love, faith and honor before the towns folks. They exchanged rings and were almost married!

Chief Thomas smiled, he looked around seeing the 'Dalmatian couple' watching the event quietly.

Thomas grinned, "Molly and Mac, Della and Todd – I now pronounce you husband and wife, let no one ever come before each other and you live together as partners. I pronounce you husband and wife. You may kiss your bride!"

Todd grabbed Della, their lips met. As he held her tightly they could see Mac and Molly begin to lick each other's mouths.

The crowd exploded with the upbeat of the little band. Everyone sought out the couple to congratulate, eat and later dance.

CPSIA information can be obtained
at www.ICGtesting.com
Printed in the USA
BVHW030534300922
648338BV00005B/20